about the author

Jean Ure was still at school when she had her first novel published. After finishing school she took on a variety of jobs to support herself while she continued to write: cook, floor-scrubber, translator, temp, trainee nurse, usherette and shop assistant. Then, after spending two years in Paris, she enrolled at the Webber-Douglas Academy of Drama where she trained as an actress.

With over seventy books under her belt, Jean is widely recognised as one of the most successful and popular authors in this country. 'Writing,' she says, 'is the only proper job I've ever had!'

Jean lives in a 300-year-old house in Croydon with her husband, seven dogs and four cats.

Also by Jean Ure
Love is Forever
Just Sixteen

ORCHARD BOOKS
96 Leonard Street,London EC2A 4XD
Orchard Books Australia
Unit 31/56 O'Riordan Street, Alexandria, NSW 2015
First published in Great Britain in 2001
A PAPERBACK ORIGINAL
Text © Jean Ure 2001
The right of Jean Ure to be identified as the author
of this work has been asserted by her in accordance with the
Copyright, Designs and Patents Act, 1988.
A CIP catalogue record for this book is available
from the British Library.
ISBN 1 84121 831 6
1 3 5 7 9 10 8 6 4 2
Printed in Great Britain

get a life!

jean ure

ORCHARD BOOKS

For Denis, with Love

chapter one

My girlfriend – her name is Rosa; she's fourteen, same age as me. But more about her later! – she says that if you're going to write a book you have to come in with a bang.

What you have to do, she says, is think of a good strong starting point. One that's really going to grab people.

A good strong starting point for this book would be when Lars Kennedy's dog came back from the Common without him. I could write:

It was a grey Friday evening in March and Lars Kennedy had taken his German Shepherd, Adolphus, for his usual walk across the common. Lars had had Dolph since he was a tiny pup. The two of them were inseparable. So everyone knew, when the dog came back without him, that there had to be something wrong.

Or maybe that is too long-winded. Maybe I should just say:

We knew that something was wrong when Lars Kennedy's dog came back from the Common without him.

It seems terrible to be fussing and bothering about how to start. It seems almost…*trivial.* But I know it is important, if people are to read the book.

Sometimes I wonder if I really want them to. It gives me a bit of a weird feeling, to be honest. The thought of total strangers reading words that I have written. All about me and Rosa, and Mum and Dad, and Lars and Noah. But I sort of think it might be important. Telling the things that happened. *How* they happened – why they happened. I guess that's one of the reasons I'm doing it. Not just to get it out of my system, but to make people sit up and think.

Some people; not all people. Some people already think. Like Rosa, for example. She is always thinking. She is a very thinking kind of person.

Rosa is not one of the people that have to be made to sit up.

But I was. And maybe that's another reason I'm doing it.

Maybe that's the real reason.

Anyway. I think what I shall do, I shall make a list of the main characters that are going to appear. This will save me having to keep breaking off to explain who people are and what they do. I hate it when things are held up by an author keeping on interrupting the story to tell you in boring detail where characters have come from and what they look like. Once I am started, I just like to carry on.

So this is what I shall say:

These are some of the people that appear in this book.

Number One.

Steven Bradbeer. My dad!

I suppose it would be true to say that my dad is quite an interesting sort of person. He is a presenter on radio. Only local radio at the moment, but that is better than a poke in the eye with a burnt stick (as my nan would say). One day, maybe, he will get a job with the BBC and will be heard by millions all over the country. He would like that. He would be famous!

In the meanwhile, he is quite famous in Crewe, which is where we live. Well, in a village just outside, to be more precise.

I think it is better to be famous in Crewe than

not to be famous at all. If you want to be famous, that is. I'm not sure that I do. But I know that Dad would enjoy it because he is always coming home and telling us how he has been stopped in the car park or in the supermarket by someone wanting his autograph, and you can tell that he is really turned on by this.

Once when we were in a restaurant – Mum and Dad, and me and Noah – a woman came up to our table, looking a bit flustered, and said 'I'm ever so sorry to trouble you, but I wonder if I could possibly have—'

Before she could finish speaking, Dad had whipped out his special signing pen and given her this charming smile that he keeps for what he calls 'his public', and said, 'My autograph? Of course you may!'

Some celebs can get quite ratty about giving autographs, but not Dad. He's dead keen! The only trouble was, this particular woman didn't want his autograph; she just wanted the salt and pepper. She didn't even know who Dad was! I think he was a bit upset about that.

But he does this programme that starts at 7 p.m. and goes through till midnight, and you have to accept that a whole load of people are going to be watching television at that time. *We* even watch television at that time. It's a bit of a sore point with Dad.

'Wonderful, isn't it?' he says, in this glum sepulchral voice. 'Even my family doesn't listen to me!'

This is why he would like to work for the BBC, so that he can be a National Figure. He has been practising doing these interviews with people where he is really rude, as he reckons this is maybe the way to get on. Like if dorks ring him up on the programme he will say, 'Oh, go away, you stupid man! I can't waste my time talking to morons like you.' Or, 'Really, madam! You obviously have the brain of a flea.'

I wouldn't ring my dad up! No way. I think it is very belittling, to treat people like that. But listeners seem to enjoy it. They ring him in droves. I can't understand it!

Anyway, that is my dad and enough about him. Now I will move on to no. 2.

Number Two is Penny Bradbeer. My mum! Also know as Penny Walker.

When she is being Penny Walker she is almost as much of a celeb as my dad. She is what is known as an agony aunt. She has a column in the local paper, and another one in a magazine, where people write in with their problems and Penny Walker gives them advice.

She also has her own programme on the radio. She goes in to the studio once a week and people ring her up to talk about the things that are worrying them. Unlike Dad, Mum is always polite and sympathetic. I'd ring Mum any time! Except that I probably wouldn't, as I'd be too embarrassed. Some of the things people talk to her about! You just wouldn't believe.

Rosa says they have no pride, but Rosa is one of those people, she is never worried by anything. She is what Mum calls 'really together'. I wish I was! I am working on it.

Number Three is Noah. Noah is my brother. He is three years older than me and I suppose we are quite close, in our own way. By which I mean, we may not very often do things together, and we don't have long heart-to-hearts, as me and Rosa do, but we love each other OK. Apart from Mum and Dad, Noah and Rosa are the only other two people in the whole world that I know I could rely on one hundred per cent. It is a comforting thought.

When I was little, and very weedy and nerdy,

Noah used to keep an eye out for me. I used to get bullied quite a lot in those days; Noah always waded in to my rescue. As soon as people discovered he was my brother, they backed off. Maybe if he hadn't been there I would have stuck up for myself a bit more. Maybe. Of course I don't know for sure; I might just have got beaten up.

When I moved from Juniors to Seniors, Noah was already there ahead of me. All the little guys in Year Seven knew who he was. Noah Bradbeer! Played for the First Eleven when he was only fourteen! Got his colours after only one season! Captain of the Under-fifteen Rugby! On the swimming team! On the fencing team!

'Why can't you be more like your brother, Brad *junior*?'

This is what a boy called Ben Arrowhead used to taunt me with. (Benjy Bonehead is how Rosa refers to him.) Sport is very important at the school I go to, and I am unfortunately not very good at it. But I wasn't ever jealous of Noah! I think perhaps sometimes I was a little bit envious; but mostly I just basked in reflected glory. It's great to have a big brother that everyone looks up to! Well, it is if you're weedy and nerdy (though I am less weedy and nerdy than I used to be).

I have just realised that I haven't actually described anyone. Physically, I mean. I haven't said what they look like, which I suppose is something that has to be done.

OK! Mum. Mum, I think, is quite glam, and young for her age. She keeps herself in trim, doing workouts and such. She says it's important, if you're a public figure.

Dad. I'm not sure how I would describe Dad. Grey-haired and jowly, but also lean and handsome. He would like that! Dad is very image-conscious.

Noah. All I can think of for Noah is that he is medium height, with brown eyes and dark hair and seems to be attractive to girls. At any rate, if the swooning and mooning is anything to go by. I think he could be classed as good-looking. I know Rosa would say that as a description this is utterly pathetic, but it is the best I can do.

I should perhaps add that we both go to a school called Hadley House. Hadley House for Boys – or Hedley Hyse as Rosa, putting on a posh voice like the Queen, is wont to call it. Rosa is always having digs at Hadley. It is pretty naff, I have to admit, but we didn't choose it. It was Mum and Dad. So Rosa needn't have a go at *me*.

I shall now move on to no. 4, which is Rosa herself.

Me and Rosa have known each other since just about for ever; she only lives around the corner. We used to play together when we were kids. Rosa once stuck a pencil down my ear because she said I was obnoxious. I used to think she was a bossy know-it-all. She still is quite bossy, but I have learnt to stand up to her.

Description. I am not sure that you could describe Rosa as pretty, exactly. Mum says she is 'arresting', meaning that she is the sort of person you have to stop and look at, like if you're on the street or something, and she happens to walk by. She has this very thin, serious face, with very dark, deep eyes and very long black hair, and this extremely intense expression, like she's always thinking about how to put the world to rights. Oh, and perhaps I should also say that she is quite tall, and sort of bony. Well, slim maybe is what I should say. She is certainly not *fat*.

I reckon that's a pretty good description, myself. I just hope she approves. I think she will like the bit about her thinking how to put the world to rights. And she is not at all vain, so probably won't mind me saying she is not pretty.

The school that Rosa goes to is Combe Cross, in Crewe. It is a comprehensive, and quite tough, but her parents don't believe in private education. They are both doctors and could easily afford it, but it is a matter of principle.

I wish Mum and Dad had this principle. If they hadn't insisted on sending me and Noah to Hadley, Lars Kennedy would probably never have entered our lives and there would be no reason for me to be writing this book.

If Lars had never come to Hadley – if me and Noah had never been at Hadley. But he did, and we are, and there is nothing now that can change what happened. All I can do is write about it. And the only way I can do that is to try and get inside the person that I was then, a year ago. Try to be thirteen years old again, without any knowledge of what is to come.

I have a feeling it will not be easy, as it is impossible to totally blot things out of your mind. But it will not work if I am for ever thinking ahead and making cryptic comments. By cryptic comments I mean remarks such as 'What I didn't realise at the time' or, 'As I was to discover later,' etc. and so on. This, I think, would be like cheating. I am going to have to watch and not do it.

I see that I have already written ten pages! Longer than the longest essay I have ever done for school. But I feel that I have reached a natural stopping place: the end of the first chapter.

Now perhaps it will start to become more like a real book.

chapter
two

Now I have to find a way to start Chapter Two. I hope the beginning of every chapter isn't going to cause as many problems as the beginning of the whole book. Surely you don't have to keep coming in with a bang?

I think I shall start with Lars. The first time we ever met.

I feel that really I should have done a breakdown for Lars like I did for Mum and Dad, and Noah and Rosa. I tried, as a matter of fact; but I found it just so difficult! Thinking what to say. In the end I had to give up.

I didn't do one for me, either; but I am only the one who is telling the story, whereas Lars, it could be said, in many ways, is the most important person in the book, for without Lars none of the events I'm writing about would ever have happened. At the time, of course, I didn't know. But like I said in the last chapter, I am determined not to cheat. I am not going to write with hindsight. Just tell it like it was.

Like it was, was one afternoon near the start of the Christmas term. Rosa had dropped by, as she quite often does, and Mum had asked her if she was going to stay to tea. Me and Rosa are in and out of each other's houses the whole time. We were into chess in a big way back then; we used to play long-running games on our travelling chess sets, either Rosa coming round to my place or me to hers. Or sometimes we'd telephone each other with our next move. Rosa once rang in the middle of the night, which didn't please Mum and Dad too much.

So anyway, there we were in the kitchen, with Rosa chopping bread and Mum doing things with lettuce leaves and me waiting for the kettle to boil, when the back door's thrown open and Noah comes in, followed by this tall, blond, godlike guy. You could practically hear Mum's jaw hitting the table. As for Rosa, she just froze. (If you were to ask her today she would indignantly deny that she did this, but it happens to be *true*. This book is a true record, and this is the effect that Lars had on women.)

Noah said, 'Hi! We in time for tea?'

Mum swallowed – I distinctly saw her Adam's apple bounce up and down in her throat like a ping-pong ball – and went, 'Yes, of course!' in a bleaty kind of voice quite unlike the deep dark gravelly one she uses for her Ask Auntie prog.

'This is Lars,' said Noah. 'He's come to pick your brains.'

'Be my guest,' said Mum. 'If you can find any brains, you're welcome to pick them. I'm Noah's mum, by the way. It seems we don't perform introductions in this house.'

'Oh! Yeah. My mum,' said Noah. 'And this is my brother Joel, you've probably seem him around school. And this is his friend Rosa.'

I think it's silly of Rosa, pretending she didn't freeze. I mean, it's nothing to be ashamed of. Even I could see that Lars Kennedy was the sort of bloke that turns girls on. In spite of being blond, he wasn't soft looking. He had this very hawk-like face, with bright blue eyes set rather close, and very piercing. And he was tall! Girls seem to go for tall guys.

'Are you new at Hadley?' said Mum. Meaning: I'm sure I'd have noticed you if you'd been there before!

Lars had just started that term. I'd seen him once

or twice about the place. In fact Ben Arrowhead had already cracked a few crude jokes about Blond Beauty and the effect he was likely to have on a certain member of staff (who shall be nameless as I don't wish to run the risk of being sued).

'Why Hadley?' said Rosa, finding her voice. She never loses it for very long. 'Why not Combe Cross?'

'I've no idea,' said Lars. 'We just moved here from Sweden. My dad's firm opened a new branch.'

He had this faintly foreign accent. Another thing that gets them going!

'I'll tell you why not Combe,' said Noah. 'Because all you girls couldn't be trusted to keep your hands off!'

It's one of the few times I've seen Rosa blush. (Oh, yes, you *did.*) But in my opinion she asked for it.

Dad came down to join us, and Noah explained how Lars wanted to talk to him and Mum about getting into radio or TV. He was hoping to make a career of it. He'd already done some youth broadcasting in Sweden and was going to do media studies at uni.

Dad, in his testy way, said, 'What is it with this

meejya studies? In my day we were humble journalists. We had to get there without the benefit of *meejya* studies.'

'Steven, just shut up,' said Mum. 'Times have changed since we started out.' And then she turned to Lars and said, 'Frankly, with looks like yours I shouldn't have thought you'd have any difficulty. You're a dead cert for television!'

I thought how maybe one day we'd switch on and see him there, reading the news or interviewing politicians. Dad would blow a gasket.

'*Meejya* studies!'

I could just hear him.

As soon as tea was over, me and Rosa went off to our chess. We didn't talk about Lars; there wasn't any reason we should. He was in Year Eleven, the same as Noah. We were in Year Eight. Worlds apart!

After that first day, I never really gave him another thought. He lived just the other side of the Common, so I did bump into him in the village once or twice, and of course I saw him at school, when he'd nod and say 'Hi', but he never came back to the house. Mum asked Noah once, a couple of weeks later, 'What happened to that beautiful young man you brought home?'

Noah said, 'Lars? He's around.'

'How come we never see him?' said Mum. 'I thought he was a friend of yours?'

'Not specially,' said Noah. 'He just wanted to pick your brains.'

'Oh... So he won't be coming here any more? What a pity,' said Mum.

She sounded quite disappointed. It struck me, to use one of Rosa's more disgusting expressions, that maybe she'd got the hots for him. At her age! But I reckoned it was good that Lars wasn't a special mate of Noah's. I mean, not that there was anything wrong with Lars. Just that – well! He didn't seem Noah's kind of guy. He didn't play rugger or swim, or do any kind of sports at all, as far as I could tell. Plus he was into jazz in a big way. He and Dad had discovered, that day he came back with Noah, that they shared the same passion. They had discussed it in great and boring detail over the tea table. *Jazz*. Jazz is old men's stuff!

I said this to Noah.

'You go on about me and Rosa being old fogeys.' He was always pulling my leg about it. Calling us brain freaks and boffins. 'What about him?'

'What about who?' said Noah.

'Lars Kennedy,' I said. 'Into *jazz.*'

'To each his own,' said Noah.

I can't stand jazz! It's almost worse than classical. At least as bad. I don't know how anyone can listen to it.

'You know your trouble?' said Noah. He squashed a finger against the tip of my nose. 'You're intolerant, that's your trouble. You wait till next term...Day of Difference? That'll shake you up a bit!'

The Day of Difference is what is known as a hallowed tradition at Hadley. The reason I'm telling about it is that it plays a big part in this story.

It was started some time ago, some time in the 1950s, when a survivor from the Holocaust was invited in to school to talk about what it was like to be a Jew in Hitler's Germany. Now it happens once a year. Not always Holocaust survivors; all sorts of people that society might label 'different'. The idea being that it should challenge our preconceptions and prejudices. (That is what it says in the school brochure.)

The year before, when I was in Year Seven, a guy that was paralysed had come to talk about what it was like being in a wheelchair. I'd really like to have heard that, as it's something I've often thought about. Being paralysed, I mean. Like if I were to have some kind of accident and not be able to walk any more. Like on the rugby field, where you could quite easily get your neck broken. People like Noah never seem to consider things like that, it doesn't seem to bother them. It bothers me! I think about it all the time. I mean, we've got guys in our year the size of carthorses. Ben Arrowhead, for one.

Anyway, I didn't get to hear the paralysed guy because it's only Year Eight that get talked to. We were hoping this year it might be a transvestite, or someone that had had a sex change operation. I mean, we'd never had one, so it was about time. I mentioned this to Noah, and he said, 'Dream on! Fanny would sooner commit hara-kiri than let a transvestite into school.'

Fanny was our headmaster. We called him Fanny on account of his name being Fanshawe. What made it funny was that he was this great big bruiser of a bloke. Six foot tall and full of burst blood vessels. Dad once said he looked like a side of beef. He was your actual fundamental redneck. Show him a transvestite, he'd want to drown them in a bucket. Something to do with Christian morality. I mean, Hadley is a Christian school, and Fanny was a real hard-line Tory type. A real flat-earther. I'm not sure he even accepted that we'd descended from apes. So I guess it wasn't really on the cards he'd let anyone seriously freaky come through the doors. Not that *I'm* saying it's freaky to be transsexual. But pretty damn interesting!

'As a matter of fact, I happen to know who's coming to talk to you,' said Noah. I immediately said, 'Who?'

'Not saying! It's a secret. But it's a woman, I'll tell you that much.'

'A woman that used to be a man?' I said, hopefully.

'A woman that'll give you lot a rough time!'

'A lesbian!' I cried.

'For heaven's sake,' said Noah. 'You are just so prejudiced!'

He wouldn't say any more. I discussed it with Rosa as we came back from town one Saturday afternoon. We were strolling through the woods at the time. We liked to go through the woods as it meant we could hold hands without running the risk of being seen. (When I say seen, I mean by dorks such as Ben Arrowhead. It was only recently we'd got into the hand-holding thing. We were still a bit self-conscious about it. Even Rosa.)

'Why do you think she might be a lesbian?' said Rosa. 'Simply because Noah said she'd give you a rough time?'

'Oh! I dunno.' I humped a shoulder. It was just a smart remark, to tell you the truth.

'Are you trying to say that *normal* women wouldn't be capable of it?'

The way she said normal, all in quotes and full of heavy meaning, told me that she was just spoiling for an argument.

'I was hoping she might have had a sex change,' I said.

'You were hoping she might have hair on her chest or—'

Rosa didn't get round to telling me what else I was hoping she might have, which was probably just as well as it was bound to have been vulgar. She kind of squawked to a standstill as the undergrowth suddenly erupted and this huge hairy *thing* came bursting out and hurled itself at us. Rosa screeched and scuttled behind me. ('Well,' she said later, 'you're bigger than I am!')

Fortunately, although it looked pretty fierce the thing turned out to be quite friendly. It was this enormous German Shepherd; pure white, with a thick shaggy coat. We heard a voice call, 'Dolph! Where are you?' and Lars Kennedy also came crashing out through the undergrowth. I couldn't help thinking that he looked shifty. Well, that was just my opinion. It is not one that Rosa shares.

'Oh! Hi,' he said, when he saw me and Rosa. 'Sorry about that. Dolph! Heel! I hope he didn't frighten you?'

'Not at all,' said Rosa, lying through her teeth.

'He's actually a big softie.'

'Oh, we could see that,' said Rosa.

'I've had him since he was a pup. Come and say hallo! He won't bite.'

Well, of course, she had to, didn't she? Say hello to him, I mean. After all that big show. But it was quite true; old Dolph was soft as butter.

'Oh, he's so beeeeeeeeeautiful,' crooned Rosa, in what I personally thought was rather a sickly fashion, especially for one who is normally a cat person and says that dogs are intellectually challenged. What it was, though she would deny it, she was just trying to make a good impression. (Oh, yes, you were! Who's writing this book, anyway?)

Lars seemed quite eager to talk about his dog.

'If they hadn't changed the quarantine laws, I wouldn't have come here,' he told us. 'No way would I have put this boy in kennels for six months!'

He was nuts about old Dolph, and he didn't mind you knowing. Rosa, as the two of us walked on, said she thought that was really nice.

'What?' I said. 'Being nuts about his dog?'

'Not being *ashamed* of being nuts about his dog. Not being ashamed to show his feelings. I think more men should be like that,' said Rosa.

'What d'you think he was doing in the bushes?' I said.

Rosa giggled. 'Having a pee, probably!'

'Why go into the bushes? Why not just go behind a tree? I think there was someone in there with him,' I said.

'Ooh!' Rosa's eyes went big with pretend shock. 'You think he was making out with someone? Who could it be?' And then she giggled again and said, 'Your mum, maybe!'

I said, *'My mum?'* I was outraged, if you want to know the truth.

'Well, we know she fancies him,' said Rosa.

I could feel my face growing hot. I knew she was only winding me up, but I don't think people ought to go round casting aspersions on people's mums like that.

'My mum does not fancy Lars Kennedy!' I hissed.

'She said she did.'

'She was only kidding!'

'You reckon?' said Rosa.

'Course she was!'

Noah had said to Mum, just the other day – in front of Rosa unfortunately – that 'her favourite guy' was going to be playing a lead part in the school's end-of-term production of *Julius Caesar*.

Mum perked up immediately, though she isn't usually a great one for school productions.

'Brutus?' she said.

'Mark Antony.'

'Oh! *Friends, Romans, countrymen! Lend me your ears!*'

Mum had gone into a mock swoon. 'Such bliss! Make sure you get me a front-row ticket.'

Noah had grinned and said, 'I thought you'd want one.'

'Well, really, darling, he is so hunky! Don't you think so?'

'Don't ask me,' said Noah. 'How should I know?'

Mum had laughed and said, 'Just take it from

me…he's the cat's pyjamas! I'd share a sauna with him any time!'

But she had only been fooling around. She hadn't really meant it.

'Mums do fancy people,' said Rosa. 'Being a mum doesn't mean you're not human.'

But *Lars Kennedy?* I said this to Rosa and she said, 'What's wrong with Lars Kennedy?'

'He's creepy,' I said.

'Why? Just because he's not one of the guys?'

'No,' I said, 'because he skulks about in bushes.'

'Yeah, with your mum!'

I think I must have looked really pissed at this. I mean, there are times when that girl just goes too far. My mum and Lars Kennedy!

'Heavens, I was only *joking*,' said Rosa. 'Can't you take a joke, now?'

When I got home, the house was empty. I knew that Dad was out, 'cos he was opening a fete somewhere, and Noah was always coming and going; but I'd been expecting Mum to be there. When she wasn't, I instantly started having these ludicrous fantasies. Mum in the bushes with Lars Kennedy…Mum, having an affair.

My mum! Other people's mums might do it, like this boy at school whose mum ran off with a golf pro; but not *my* mum! She wouldn't! Surely?

Noah arrived home about half an hour after I'd got in.

'D'you know where Mum is?' I said.

'No idea. Out, I guess.'

'She didn't say she was going out!'

'So?'

'She'd have told us!'

'Maybe she's run away,' said Noah. 'Can't stand the sight of your bedroom any more.'

I scowled. Mum had been going on at me about my bedroom only that morning.

'You don't think she's eloped with Lars Kennedy?' I said. I did it just, like, half joking. But half meaning it, too! Just to see if Noah would take it seriously. See if he'd noticed anything.

To my relief, he just laughed.

'You've been watching too many soaps,' he said.

As a matter of fact, me and Rosa do not watch soaps. We are above that kind of thing. And middle-aged women *do* elope with schoolboys; in real life, I mean. You read about it all the time. But anyway, Mum came bursting in a few minutes later with her arms full of greenery.

'Table decorations!' She waved it at us. 'You haven't forgotten, boys, have you? Big night tonight! All scrubbed and polished, please. Best behaviour!'

Me and Noah looked at each other and pulled faces. Tonight was the night when the head honcho from Dad's radio station was coming to dinner. We couldn't possibly have forgotten! Dad had been wittering on about it for the past fortnight.

'There you are, you see.' Noah ruffled my hair. 'Mummy's back! No cause for alarm.'

'Who's alarmed?' said Mum.

'Joel was. Poor little diddums! He thought you'd run off with Lars.'

'With Lars?' said Mum. 'I should be so lucky!'

'You mean, you'd like to?' I said.

'Darling,' said Mum, 'who wouldn't?' She thrust the greenery at me. 'Just take these bits and pieces and put them in water for me,' she said, 'there's a good lad.'

I did what she said, but I couldn't stop my brain from going into overdrive.

Greenery.

Woods.

'Darling, who wouldn't?'

My mum is rather theatrical, as you may have noticed. She says these sort of things all the time.

But kidding! Only kidding! It doesn't do to take her seriously. Not really.

I'm thinking now of other times, in those early days, when I came into contact with Lars. Me on my own, that is, or with Rosa. I can only remember just the once, and even then I can't precisely place it. I mean, I can geographically; but not timewise. Before Christmas is the nearest I can get.

Geographically it was out near Scuppers Hill, as the road comes off the Common. I was zooming along on my bike when I saw Lars bending over something at the side of the road. Well, I saw Dolph first; he was, like, standing guard. Then I saw Lars, so I skidded to a halt. Just nosiness, really; I didn't specially want to talk to him.

'Look at this!' he said.

It was a badger. Dead, of course. The only time you ever get to see badgers, it sometimes seems to me, is when they're dead. It's a pretty sad sight, but you sort of get hardened to it. You have to; the roadside verges are littered with corpses. Badgers, foxes, rabbits: cats, squirrels. You name it, it's there. You can't afford the emotional drain of taking each one personally.

Maybe in Sweden it doesn't happen. Maybe they don't have the same kind of wildlife. Or the same amount of traffic. I don't know. Lars was really gutted. Rosa would have said it was touching, but myself, to be honest, I found it a bit embarrassing.

He started to rail on about cars and the bastards who drove them. I said, 'They come out the woods. You can't always see them.'

Lars wouldn't accept that. He said, 'There's no need for all this slaughter! It shows a total disregard for other forms of life.'

I said, 'Yeah. Well,' hoping he wasn't going to ask me to help him pick it up or anything.

I can remember him squatting there, by the side of the road, lamenting the fact that the badger was so beautiful and some bastard had had to go and terminate its life. I could see that it had really got to him.

When he'd finally finished lamenting and railing, he called to Dolph and we set off down the hill together. I'd rather have jumped back on my bike and gone on ahead, to tell the truth, but it didn't seem quite polite, especially when he was still talking.

As we walked, he told me things about himself. He told me how he'd thought of becoming a vet, but how he didn't think he'd be able to handle having to put an animal down. So then he'd thought of going into the media, in the hope that one day he'd make a name for himself as a TV personality and could maybe do wildlife programmes.

It seems kind of surprising, looking back, the fact that he talked to me. I mean, most Year Elevens wouldn't have bothered. They certainly wouldn't have told me, like Lars did, how upset he'd been when his cat was run over.

'It's a bereavement,' he said, 'when you lose an animal. People don't always realise that. But they're not just...*things*, like cabbages. They're living creatures, with their own personalities. Just as we are. They're part of the family.'

I mumbled sympathetic agreement, though in fact we've never actually had any pets as Dad is allergic. I told Lars this, and he said he didn't think he could live without what he called 'an animal companion'.

I don't remember that I gave him many details about myself, and he didn't ask. But I didn't get the impression it was because he wasn't interested; just that he reckoned, if I wanted him to know, I'd volunteer the information same as he had.

Later on I told Rosa about it, and she said that Lars sounded like a nice guy.

'Not one of your boneheads.'

I agreed that he wasn't a bonehead; and I agreed that he was a nice guy.

'But?' said Rosa.

I couldn't say there wasn't a but because there was. It was just that I didn't quite know how to put it into words. Maybe I simply wasn't used to anyone at Hadley showing signs of sensitivity. Maybe that's what it was.

Anyway, it's the only time I ever remember talking to him except once later on, which I haven't yet come to. I think I respected him all right; I think if anyone had asked me I'd have said he was OK. But mostly, to be honest, I never gave him a second's thought. I mean, he just didn't play any part in my life. Except those moments when I wondered about him and Mum…that was the thing that really bothered me.

chapter
three

Every year, at Hadley, at the end of the Christmas term, the Upper School have an Evening. Always with a different theme. Like the year before it had been the Millennium, and another year it had been Law & Order. The Law & Order Ball, with everyone dressed up as crooks and coppers.

This year it was to be a Victorian Evening, and me and Rosa were dying to know who Noah was going to take with him. Well, Rosa was dying to know. I was mildly curious, is the way I would put it.

I don't mean to be sexist here, but this kind of thing – girlfriends, boyfriends, who's going out with who – really seems to give girls a buzz. Even serious-minded ones like Rosa. I was quite surprised, to tell you the truth. I'd have thought she was above all that stuff.

'What do you mean?' she said. *'That stuff?* We're

talking human relationships here!'

'We're talking vulgar curiosity,' I said.

'There's nothing vulgar about it! It's perfectly natural to be interested. He's your brother, isn't he?'

'I don't reckon he'd be very intcrested in knowing who I was taking.'

'No, because he'd know you'd be taking me! You would be, wouldn't you?' She squared up to me, all pugnacious, thrusting her face into mine. She can be quite aggressive, Rosa can. 'You havcn't got any other girlfriends hidden away?'

'Course I haven't!' I nearly added, 'You're as much as I can cope with,' but I thought perhaps she might not find it funny. On the other hand, she might have done. You can't always tell. Most of the time we share the same sense of humour and laugh at the same kind of jokes, but just now and again I'll go and put my foot in it. Sometimes, with girls, you have to tread a bit carefully.

'Noah hasn't got anyone steady, has he?' said Rosa.

'Not's far as I know,' I said.

'So who d'you think it'll be?'

'Dunno.'

'I think he'll take Emily Whitchurch.'

Emily Whitchurch is this girl that lives just

outside our village and goes to the same school as Rosa, except three years higher up. She's like a sort of female version of Lars Kennedy. Mum calls her the Blonde Bombshell. All the guys fancy her.

'She'd go if he asked her,' said Rosa. 'She'd go like a shot!'

I said, 'How d'you know?'

''Cos her cousin's in my class and she told me. She said Emily's crazy about him.'

'What, about Noah? She went with Richard Benyon last year.'

'That was only because it was the Millennium Ball and she was desperate to go and he was head boy. He was a creep! She'd far rather have gone with Noah. She's just waiting for him to ask her!'

All I did was grunt, 'cos like I said I wasn't all that interested, really, who Noah took to the Victorian Evening with him. He went out with different girls all the time. But Rosa, she's one of those people, she can't let a subject drop. Not till she's beaten it and battered it and shaken it about. She must have gone through about a dozen girls before finally coming back to Emily Whitchurch.

'I reckon she's the one. Why don't you try asking him?'

'Me?' I said. 'Why me? You're the one that wants to know. You ask him!'

'I couldn't,' said Rosa; and she gave this little giggle, all girlish and silly. 'He might think I'm hinting.'

'Hinting what?'

'That he ought to take me!'

Take Rosa? 'He wouldn't do that,' I said.

'Why not?' Now she'd gone all aggressive again. All bristling.

'Well—' I waved a hand. I knew I had to be careful. She might take offence if I said the idea was ludicrous. I mean…Noah and Rosa! But I didn't want to upset her.

'You're my girlfriend,' I said. 'It wouldn't occur to him.'

'Well, but I still couldn't ask him. You could! You're his brother.'

'Yeah, but we don't talk about things like that,' I said.

Me and Noah, we never discuss personal matters. We have more of a joky-joky kind of relationship. Like one of us might say, 'Watch out! Mum's about! She's in a right mood.' Or, 'Steer clear of Dad, he's having an identity crisis…no one's asked for his autograph for forty-eight hours.' That kind of thing. Never girlfriends.

Rosa sighed. 'Well, if you won't, you won't,' she said. 'But I think it's very unenterprising of you.'

It turned out Rosa wasn't the only one suffering from vulgar curiosity. Mum was too.

'Come on, then!' she said, over supper one evening. 'Spill the beans! Who's the lucky girl?'

'Lucky in what way?' said Noah.

'Don't come that with me!' Mum wagged a finger at him. 'You know perfectly well what I'm talking about!'

Noah spread his hands. He looked at me, eyebrows raised.

'She means who are you taking to the Victorian Evening,' I said.

'Oh! That. I'm doing my best to get out of it,' said Noah.

'What?' Mum stared at him. 'Get out of it? You can't be serious! Of course you're not getting out of it. What would I do for gossip?'

Mum adores gossip; so does Dad. Mum likes to know who's going out with whom, who's having babies, who's having affairs, who's getting married. Dad's more into conspiracies. He has this persecution complex (that's what Mum says) and thinks everyone's plotting against him. So he likes to know who's talking to whom and what they're talking about.

Me and Noah aren't really into all that. Mum's for ever complaining that we don't bring her enough gossip.

'Where are all the juicy bits?' she goes. 'I want the juicy bits!'

'If you want to know,' said Noah, 'I think the whole idea of a Victorian Evening is pathetic.'

But he had to go, because it was expected of him. He came home the next day grumbling about it.

'You'll have to learn some Victorian dance steps,' I said. 'You'll have to learn how to polka!'

'*Polka?* Are you out of your skull?' said Noah.

'No! It's what they did.'

'Absolutely!' said Mum. 'You'd better be prepared. Polkas, waltzes, Dashing White Sergeant...'

'I'm not going to be doing any of that crap,' said Noah. 'I'm just going to skulk in a corner.'

Mum pounced. 'Ah! But who are you going to skulk with? That's the question!'

'Emily Whitchurch,' I said. Even I was starting to get a bit interested.

'The Bombshell?' said Mum. 'She won't be content to skulk!'

I went round to Rosa and told her that I reckoned she was right.

'I reckon it's Emily Whitchurch.'

'I knew it, I knew it!' crowed Rosa.

But it wasn't Emily Whitchurch. It was someone totally unexpected. It was this girl called Anna that lives with her mum and dad in the old farmhouse up the hill, at the far end of the village. How we found out, Anna's mum called round one afternoon when me and Mum were alone, having our tea. Mum invited her in, and she came and sat down and just burst out with it.

'Did you know that Noah has asked Anna to go to the Victorian Evening with him?'

There was a pause. Mum didn't exactly freeze in mid-air with her cup half way to her mouth, but you could tell that she was a bit – well! Taken aback. I was, too. I mean, Anna is a very sweet person and Noah has always had a soft spot for her, but she is older than him by three years and she has the mental age of a small child. When she was fourteen and me and Rosa were still at Infants, she used to play with us in the sandpit in Rosa's back garden.

Noah had gone to her rescue one day when some yobs were making fun of her, and from then on she'd had this huge crush on him. If ever she saw him anywhere, like in the village or at a school fete, she'd make a beeline straight for him. She'd attach herself, like a little dog, and follow him round. I'd have been dead embarrassed, but Noah never seemed to mind. And now he'd gone and invited her to the Victorian Evening!

Mum swallowed and said, 'I didn't know.'

'Well, he has, apparently. So Anna says.'

'You don't think…' Mum hesitated. I could see she was trying to choose her words. 'You don't think she's…misunderstood?'

'That's exactly what I did think! But she claims they've already discussed what time he's going to pick her up. She says he's promised to teach her how to dance, he's going to bring her back afterwards, and now she's clamouring to go into town and buy a dress to wear. So I don't know what to make of it!'

Slowly, Mum said, 'I'll check with Noah.'

'I would be grateful. She's so excited! She's over the moon. If it were anyone but Noah, I'd think it was just a cruel joke.'

'No.' Mum shook her head. 'Noah wouldn't do a thing like that. But I'll check it's not some kind of misunderstanding.'

I reckoned it had to be, and I'm pretty sure Mum did, too. Anna's very suggestible, you can tell her anything and she'll believe it. Or else she gets these ideas into her head and nothing will shift them.

'That poor girl!' said Mum. 'If she's got hold of the wrong end of the stick it's going to break her heart!'

Mum taxed Noah with it the minute he got in, which was about twenty minutes after Anna's mum had left.

'What's all that about Anna thinking she's going to the Victorian Evening with you?'

'She is,' said Noah. 'I asked her.'

'You asked *Anna*?' That was me. I just couldn't believe it! I couldn't believe that my brother was going to the Victorian Evening with someone that was mentally handicapped.

I expect that sounds quite bad, actually. But it was how I felt.

Very calmly, Noah said, 'Why shouldn't I ask Anna? No one else is likely to.'

'You should have asked Emily! She's just dying to go with you!'

'Emily can get anyone she wants. She'll always be the centre of attention.'

'Yes, but—'

'But what?'

But Anna's simple, is what I wanted to say. She's not all there! She's quite prettyish, but kind of…vacant-looking. What I mean is, you can tell at a glance she's one slice short of a sandwich. The truth was, I didn't like the idea of people seeing her with Noah and maybe thinking that's all he could get. But I couldn't very well say it.

'Look, I didn't want to go to the thing anyway,' said Noah. 'But if I've got to, then why shouldn't I take Anna and make her happy?'

'Oh, it's making her happy all right,' said Mum. 'It's making her delirious!'

'So what's the problem?'

'I'm just worried. In case—'

'In case what?'

'Young people can be very unkind,' said Mum.

'So can old people!'

'True. *People* can be very unkind. But young people don't always think.'

'What exactly are you trying to say?' said Noah.

'I'm trying to say that Anna is very vulnerable and I don't want her to get hurt!'

'She won't get hurt,' said Noah. 'I won't let her.'

'Well, you make sure you don't.'

'I won't! I want her to enjoy herself. One of us might as well. I want to make this something special for her.'

'Yes, and then she'll follow you round even more than she does already,' I said.

'So what? It's nothing I can't handle. You get on with your life,' said Noah, 'and I'll get on with mine.'

As soon as I'd finished my homework I rushed round to break the news to Rosa. I thought she'd be as put out as I was, but instead she cried, 'Oh! That's brilliant!' She is always surprising me.

'I don't see what's brilliant about it,' I said. I was not best pleased, to be honest. I said this to Rosa. I said, 'He could ask any girl he wanted! And he has to go and choose *Anna*.'

'But don't you see?' said Rosa. 'That's why it's so brilliant! It's a gesture. Noah's one of the few people that could get away with it. Because everyone *knows* he could ask any girl he wanted. I think you should be proud of him!'

Maybe I should have been. Well, I *know* I should have been. It was a very brave and admirable thing to do, inviting Anna to be his partner. But next day Ben Arrowhead came up to me, his face all gloating, and said, 'Guess who my brother's going

to the Victorian Evening with? Emily Whitchurch!
Whey-hey!'

Like Noah couldn't have gone with her if he'd
wanted to. Like he wouldn't have been her first
choice.

I was pretty mad at him, to tell the truth.

chapter
four

Christmas.

Christmas in our house is a somewhat strange experience; at least, that's how it's always seemed to me. For a start we don't go to church, not even for the carols or the midnight service, on account of Mum and Dad being very strongly not religious. Dad especially. I think Mum might go, just for the sake of goodwill, what with the Vicar living across the road and all, but Dad tends to get a bit aerated on the subject, so as usual Mum gives in. Anything for a quiet life, is what she says.

I don't expect, probably, that most people go to church at Christmas, not these days, but in a village like ours it's more of a social occasion, like just about *everybody* goes on Christmas Eve. Rosa doesn't, but that's because her family are Jewish. They don't really keep Christmas, though me and

Rosa always give each other presents. The Christmas I'm writing about I gave her a CD of some of her favourite music, which is Bach, if you can believe that. (It's because she plays him on the piano.) I don't know how we'd get on if we were married because I can't stand classical music!

What Rosa gave me was a copy of this book she'd discovered called *Catcher in the Rye*. It's brilliant! Really funny, but kind of sad at the same time. Rosa always gives good presents.

Anyway, the reason I reckon our Christmas is strange is that we don't seem to do any of the things that normal people do. Like for instance we don't watch television because Dad says it's moronic and if we can't live without it for just two days of the year it means our brains must be frazzled. So the television's locked away in a cupboard (to remove temptation) and no one's allowed to go near it.

Then another thing! We don't have a Christmas tree because Mum and Dad fell out over whether it was ecologically sounder to get a real one or a fake one. They had *words* about it. So no more Christmas tree!

Plus we don't have decorations ever since Dad

put them up one year and Mum scoffed and said, 'Well, that's original!' to which Dad took great exception. What he'd done was just loop these long concertinas of red and green hoops from the corners of the room up to the light fitting in the middle. It was pretty naff, I have to agree, but Dad got mad as a hornet and went off in a sulk saying that if Mum didn't like it she could do it herself. So now nobody does it. Dad won't, on principle. (He can be quite childish.) Mum won't, on some other kind of principle. (She can also be quite childish.) Me and Noah could if we wanted, but somehow we never do. Rosa did it one year, when she was still in Juniors and enjoyed making Chinese lanterns and paper chains, but she's grown out of that now. So Mum has dead twig arrangements, instead. She says it's more classy.

Another thing we don't get to do is eat Christmas dinner. Well, not the sort of Christmas dinner that everyone else eats. What we have – this'll kill you! – what we have is nut loaf and champagne. We're not specially veggie the rest of the year, but Mum says on Christmas Day we ought not to consume slaughtered animal, and it doesn't matter how much Dad grumbles, he has to go along with it. She's loopy, at times, my Mum!

Rosa, of course thinks it's great, because Rosa never eats meat anyway. (Which is another thing: what would we do about food? If we were married, that is. She's veggie and I'm a carnivore! It would never work.)

The big happening in our house, on Christmas Day, is the arrival of what Dad calls the Horde. The horde is Uncle Glenn and Auntie Megan plus Chloë, Fiona and the twins. Auntie Megan is Mum's sister. She is very like Mum both to look at and in character. She and Mum tend to do rather a lot of girlish giggling when they are together. Dad and Uncle Glenn are also quite ho-ho-ish with one another. After two bottles of champagne they get all chummy and blokeish and start telling these manly kind of jokes that the girls aren't supposed to listen to, though naturally they always do.

Fiona is two years older than Noah, and Chloë is two years younger. The twins are mere infants. Auntie Megan says they were an afterthought, though Mum thinks they were a mistake. I hope Mum never makes a mistake! She's too old for that sort of thing and I don't think I could cope with a baby – or worse still, babies! – in the house.

As well as the Horde we also have the Brissetts.

Mr and Mrs. They are this aged old couple that live next door. Dad calls them the Wee Folk. They are really dorky, but kind of funny. They do this double act where they echo each other. Like Mrs B. might say, 'We went down the shops the other day.' And Mr B. will say, 'Other day.'

'Must have been Thursday.'

'Thursday.'

'No, wait! I tell a lie!'

'Tell a lie.'

'Thursday was the day Iris came.'

'Iris came.'

'Brought those flowers.'

'Those flowers.'

It kills me when they go on like that! It drives Dad demented. You can see him getting all twitchy, and you know that what he'd really like to do would be to yell at them like he yells at the people on his programme.

'Stop blethering, you morons!'

He doesn't, of course, because Mum would be mad at him. She says once a year he can learn to be tolerant. I don't know why he doesn't just sit back and enjoy it, but sometimes I think perhaps Dad doesn't have too much sense of humour.

This particular Christmas, the one I'm talking

about, which was Christmas last year, was just about the same as all other Christmases except that Fiona didn't come on account of spending the day with her boyfriend. Mum was immediately interested!

'Boyfriend?' she says. 'On Christmas Day? This sounds serious!'

So then they start talking about it, and Auntie Megan says how she met him at uni and how she's fallen for him in a big way, and how lovely it must be to be young and in love, and Mum shrieks, 'Oh! Do you remember? William Bagley?' which was some kind of nerd Mum once went out with, and I've heard it all before so I tune out of that conversation and tune in to another one that's taking place between Noah and Chloë, but that's just as excruciating as Mum and Auntie Megan's.

Chloë's got this huge big thing about Noah. She's always had it, but just recently it's got worse. It's love's young dream, according to Mum, and it would be all right if Noah had it in return, but he's not really interested in her. I don't know why not, as she's quite cute and she's doing her best to get him going. As an outside observer, I can see it all. She's making a dead set at him! Big owly eyes and girly giggles and lots of unnecessary touching, on account of Mum, ever hopeful, has sat them next to each other. (Mum is into romance in a big way. She'd like all the world to be in love.)

Noah's not really responding. I mean, he's not giving her the brush-off, or anything like that; he's just not turned on. Maybe it's because they've known each other since they were in their prams. But so have me and Rosa! On the other hand I'm not sure how I'd react if Rosa started going all girlish and soppy. I'm not sure I'd like it. I think it might embarrass me!

I sat and studied Noah, trying to work out if he was embarrassed. He didn't seem to be. Nothing very much embarrasses Noah, and anyway, he was used to it. Dad once said he must have been out with every girl between here and Nantwich. Except for Emily Whitchurch. I still didn't understand that. I mean, by all accounts she was willing.

'How about Noah?' Auntie Megan's voice suddenly came fluting across the table.

'Noah!' One of the Wee Folk. They sometimes echo other people as well as each other.

'Who's the latest lady love?'

'Lady love.'

'Looks like someone pretty close to him,' said

Dad; and he and Uncle Glenn gave these macho chuckles.

Old Chloë, she blushed like crazy, but you could tell she was basking in it. I mean, she really liked the idea of people thinking she was Noah's girlfriend. Noah didn't blush because he doesn't. He's lucky. I wish I didn't.

I *really* wish I didn't. 'Cos next thing I know, they've started on me. It's Noah that's done it.

'If you want to know about lady loves,' he says, 'try asking my young stud of a brother! A right little goer, aren't you?'

And there's me, lit up like a beacon, and Noah grinning all over his face 'cos he's got them off of his back and on to mine, and Auntie Megan's leaning forward, all agog, across the table. She's as bad as Mum when it comes to gossip.

'What's this, what's this?' she goes. 'Girlfriends at his age?'

'It's only Rosa,' goes Mum.

'Only Rosa,' go the Wee Folk. (They do it in chorus, sometimes.)

'Oh! Rosa.' Auntie Megan knows Rosa. She's known her for years. You can tell she's a bit disappointed. She'd been hoping for something more exciting!

'They're into chess at the moment,' says Noah. He kicks me under the table. *'Aren't you?'*

I scowl at him, and he winks, and kicks me again.

'Chess?'

Suddenly I get the message. We're doing a Wee Folk!

'Yeah, yeah! Chess,' I say.

'King's pawn to Rook Three—'

'Rook Three.' He hasn't the faintest idea what he's talking about. But at least it's got us off the girlfriend kick.

I hate it when grown-ups pretend to take an interest when really they're just using it as an excuse to have a laugh. I know they don't mean to be hurtful; I know they think it's really amusing. But it's an extremely irritating habit and one that I am definitely not going to indulge in when I am grown-up. I shall treat young people with *respect*.

After we'd finished dinner, Dad wanted to start playing games. Dad really loves games! Charades, forfeits, Twenty Questions. All that sort of stuff. I don't mind it. Rosa always comes round, 'cos she loves it just as much as Dad. They really egg each other on! We have quite good fun, though sometimes it can get a bit heavy, like if Dad thinks people aren't taking it seriously enough.

When the knock at the door came Mum chirruped, 'That'll be his lady love!' Meaning Rosa. She doesn't usually tease me like that, she's usually more sensible. She was just doing it because of Auntie Megan being there.

'My playmate!' said Dad. 'Good! Now we can get started.'

But it wasn't Rosa, it was Lars and Dolph. Lars explained that he'd been taking Dolph for a walk across the Common and thought he'd drop by to wish us a happy Christmas.

'Well, come in!' cried Mum, practically yanking him through to the sitting room. I could see Auntie Megan's eyes going like saucers.

It must be strange, I think, to have this effect on women. I am not sure that I could handle it, though fortunately there is not much danger of me having to.

'Introduce us!' cried Auntie Megan. They're very forward, these older women.

'Lars, this is my sister Megan,' said Mum. 'Her husband Glenn. Chloë—'

Chloë beamed and blushed and sort of scrunched herself up closer to Noah. I saw Noah send this comical drowning-man-in-distress look at Lars, and Lars half raise an eyebrow and grin. I think I was the only one that saw it. I guess Lars knew what Noah was suffering. He must have suffered it himself most of the time.

'And these are our next-door neighbours,' said Mum. 'Mr and Mrs Brissett.'

'Brissett.'

'This is Noah's friend from school…Lars.'

'Very pleased to meet you, Lars.'

'Meet you, Lars.'

Chloë suddenly giggled and buried her head in Noah's shoulder. I felt quite embarrassed for him, to tell you the honest truth. I wouldn't even want Rosa doing that! I mean, not in public.

Lars only stayed just a short time. Dad wanted to rope him in to play games, but he excused himself. He said he had to be getting back.

'How wise!' murmured Mum.

Mum enjoys playing Dad's games just as much as anyone else, so I don't know why she said that. Rosa says it's because grown-ups can't always admit to enjoying childish things. They have to make like they're only doing them on sufferance.

'That's what's good about your dad. He's not ashamed to admit it!'

He's not only not ashamed, he wallows in it. He just loves to get us all organised! Teams, and sides, and pencils and paper. He tried his best to talk Lars into staying, but Lars said his mum would be wondering where he was.

'So ring her!' said Dad.

'Yes, ring her, ring her!' That was Auntie Megan, joining in. She was even worse than Mum!

But Lars glanced at Noah and I saw Noah pull a face. I guess he was trying to warn Lars that playing games in our house is not something to be taken lightly. To Dad, games are a serious business. To Rosa, too. If anyone cheats or starts goofing around, beware! You're in trouble.

So Lars said he was sorry, but he really did have to go; and Noah then jumped up and said that he would go with him.

'What, now?' said Dad. He couldn't believe it! Noah going off for a walk when he could be here, playing games?

'Start without me,' said Noah. 'I'll be back.'

'Can I come with you?' Old Chloë had sprung to her feet, all bright and beaming.

There was a pause.

'It's pretty muddy over the Common,' said Noah.

Chloë's face fell.

'That's all right! She can have my wellies. Joel—'

Mum gave me a little push. 'Go and get my wellies!'

I tell you, she'll do anything to encourage romance, my mum will. She thought it was really sweet, the way old Chloë kept cosying up to Noah. She couldn't understand why he didn't respond.

'She's such a dear little thing!'

But Mum ought to know, as an agony aunt, that it's not just a question of being a dear little thing. It's a question of chemistry. You've either got it, or you haven't. Now, me and Rosa, we might almost have come out of the same test tube, we get on so well together. But you can't force people. Mum ought to know that.

Anyway, the problem was solved by Mum's wellies being way to big for Chloë's feet. For a moment it looked like she was so fixated she'd be willing to slop across the Common in her slippers, until I pointed out that the place in fact was like a bog.

I don't know why I did it, really; it's not like I was in Noah's debt or anything. But he winked and whispered, 'Owe you one!' as he went off with Lars, and I guess I quite liked it, the feeling it gave me. Like him and me were in some kind of conspiracy together.

Auntie Megan could hardly wait for the door to close before she came bursting out with it.

'Well! And what was that? The new Brad Pitt???'

'Gorgeous, or what?' said Mum.

'Or what!' said Auntie Megan. She giggled. 'I wouldn't mind having him as a strippergram for my birthday!'

'I saw him first,' said Mum.

Honestly! The way they carried on. And Dad and Uncle Glenn just sitting there knocking back the champagne, not turning a hair. Not that Uncle Glenn has much hair to turn. But Dad has! I couldn't understand how he could be so cool about it. I mean, Mum…his wife! Lusting after young flesh.

It was over an hour before Noah came back. Dad was fretting and fuming 'cos he thought he was trying to avoid playing charades. I thought it was more likely he was trying to avoid Chloë. I mean, she was being so obvious it was pathetic. (But with Auntie Megan for a mum, and my mum for an aunt, how could you blame her?)

'Where have you been?' said Dad. 'I'm trying to arrange teams!'

'Sorry, sorry!' said Noah. 'We went over the golf course.'

'Well, go and sit there, next to Chloë. It's…'

'Noah! Dear heart! Tell me something!' That

was Auntie Megan, swooping across the room. Clasping her arms round Noah's neck. Theatricality seems to run in Mum's side of the family. 'Put us out of our misery! We want to know…does your friend strip?'

'Sorry?' said Noah. It's one of the few times I've ever seem him taken aback. He's pretty cool, as a rule.

'Strip!' squawked Auntie Megan. 'Does he strip? Your mum and I want him for our birthdays…we fancy him like crazy!'

'We do,' said Mum. 'But I'm having him first!'

Rosa and I discussed it later.

'I can see why you think it's funny,' I said. 'But I don't reckon you'd be laughing if it were your mum!'

'Oh, rats!' said Rosa. 'Anyway, it wouldn't *be* my mum. She had me rather late in life. She's past it. Your mum's in her sexual prime.'

'She's what?' I said. I couldn't believe I was hearing this!

'She's in her sexual prime…mine's having hot flushes. Yours is still young. Well…youngish. Young enough' – Rosa giggled – 'to fancy Lars Kennedy!'

It brought back all the worries that I'd been trying to bury. Mum and Lars Kennedy…how could she be so *blatant* about it? It could only mean one thing: Dad didn't care any more. Neither of them cared! The marriage was over!

I know this sounds really wimpish, but I have always had this secret fear that one day Mum and Dad would break up. After all, they are both career people, and they are both ambitious; and Dad is self-centred, and Mum is – well! The sort of person that flirts at parties. Also they are celebs, even if only minor ones. Celebs, it seems to me, go in for divorce in a big way. Serial marriage. They collect partners the way other people collect stamps.

I poured out my worries to Rosa, and this time she didn't laugh. She took me quite seriously. Solemnly she said, 'It is always possible that your mum is going through a mid-life crisis.'

What did this mean???

'You don't *really* think she'd want to have it off with Lars?' I said.

'Well, look at it this way…What we have to ask ourselves is, why did he come round today? Was it really to say 'Happy Christmas', or was it to see your mum?'

Glumly I said that I could see no reason why Lars Kennedy should want to drop by just to say happy Christmas.

'Considering he hardly knows us. He hardly even knows Noah. I mean, they don't hang out or anything. They're not particularly friends.'

'Hm. Sounds bad,' said Rosa. 'We shall have to keep an eye on the situation!'

chapter
five

The next important significant thing that happened in our lives was New Year's. Back when it was the Millennium, our village and all the surrounding villages linked up to have a Millennium bash. It was such a success they decided to have one every year. It was held at the top of Fidler's Hill – well, the fireworks were set off on Fidler's Hill; the actual party was held in the Grand Assembly Rooms in the village. Everybody went! Rosa and her mum and dad. The Wee Folk. The Vicar. Emily Whitchurch. Ben Arrowhead. Lars Kennedy. Mum and Dad. Me and Noah. Everybody!

As a rule, Dad sneers at what he calls mass entertainment, meaning anything that appeals to the sort of people that ring him up on his programme and that he abuses and calls morons.

He likes to think he's above all the rest of humanity. But it's different when he's made Master of Ceremonies! Which is what he is at New Year's. There are lots of people far grander than Dad that live around here, I mean doctors and lawyers and architects and such; but Dad's the local celeb. When he picks up the mike and goes, 'Ladies and gentlemen!' everyone recognises him as Steven Bradbeer.

'You know! The rude one.'

He's not rude at New Year's, of course. He's usually had a bit to drink, which means he's very jolly and ho-ho-ho-ish. It used to embarrass me when I was younger, but I guess I've got used to it now. Noah says it's his professional persona and it's what the public like. You have to give the public what they like or you don't get to be a celeb. This is just one of the reasons why I probably shan't ever be one.

So, anyway. We went to New Year's and everybody was there and Dad was on top form, ho-ho-ho-ing like mad, all full of benevolence and bonhomie, and it was great and it was brilliant and it was absolutely ace. But the very best thing of all was this: me and Rosa had our first kiss…

Our first *real* kiss. With all the tongue stuff, and

that. Stuff I'd only read about. It was like rockets exploding in your head. It was like…intoxicating! It's not something you can ever imagine. It's something you have to experience.

It didn't happen at the stroke of midnight, when traditionally everyone goes kissy kissy, huggy huggy. I mean, me and Rosa went kissy huggy along with all the rest, but that was only normal, polite, everyday kissy huggy. The sort of kissy huggy you could do in a shopping mall, for instance, and not get arrested for. The real stuff – the hard stuff! – that happened afterwards.

We'd both had a glass of punch, but we weren't drunk. No way! We'd gone outside to watch the fireworks and got into a clinch on account of it was really cold, in spite of a huge great bonfire and us being all wrapped up in several layers of clothing. Everybody was stamping, and hugging themselves. Me and Rosa just hugged each other, and – well! That was when it happened.

Our lips met. And instead of staying closed and pinched and prunelike, they opened up – like sea anemones, is how I like to think of it – and for just a few rapturous moments we kissed the world away. Truly, we became a part of each other. Her lips to my lips: my lips to hers. Nobody else mattered. Nobody else even existed. I forgot we were in a public place with many beady and curious eyes fixed upon us. (Eyes such as Ben Arrowhead's, as I discovered later, to my cost.) It was just me and Rosa, in a world of our own. Our own private time bubble. (I picture it as being a bit like a cod-liver oil capsule.) Body to body, mouth to mouth...

You have to have the right person for it, of course. I cannot for instance imagine pressing lips with Polly Bunsen, who is a girl that used to go to our ballroom dancing classes and was somewhat like a pudding, though that was probably to do with her genes and should not be held against her. It's just that she didn't turn me on. But upon reflection I probably didn't turn her on, either.

All I will say is that if you get the right person, then to kiss is bliss!

I can't understand, now, how we left it so long. I mean, me and Rosa, we'd been best buddies for ever! Maybe that was it. Maybe we were too used to each other. We were just, like...old mates. Until that moment on Fidler's Hill, when suddenly – wham! Everything changed.

Sadly, all good things come to an end (as the saying goes). Even a kiss has a limited life span.

Alas! Our lips came apart with a sort of gluggy noise. We had been glued so tight together! I felt very moved and told Rosa that I would love her till the end of time. Rosa said that she would love me till the end of time, too.

'I will love you for millennia,' I said.

Rosa looked a bit solemn at this.

'Do you realise,' she said, 'that when they hold the next millennium celebrations we'll have been dead for *centuries?*'

It was a sobering thought. The crowds of the future gathered on Fidler's Hill to usher in the Year 3,000 and me and Rosa not amongst them! But I didn't want to be sad.

'Our spirits will still be around...they'll roam the universe, locked in eternal embrace.'

I meant it quite seriously. Rather poetic, I thought. (I still do.) But Rosa suddenly giggled. She is like that. She giggles at the most inopportune moments. Her sense of humour is very unpredictable. I expect it is part of the reason that I love her.

'I'm not laughing because it's funny,' she told me. 'I'm laughing because it's *delicious!*'

So that was all right!

Being in love, I have discovered, is a bit like

bouncing about on a trampoline. You have to be careful or you can lose control and go flying up so high you're in danger of never coming down. Like your head's in the clouds and there's nothing to keep you anchored. You lose touch with reality! Nothing can get through to you. Not even a Neanderthal nerd like Ben Arrowhead.

'Saw you New Year's Eve, Jo-ly!' It's his idea of a joke, calling me Joly. 'Sucking and blowing like a vacuum cleaner!' And then he makes these sucky blowy noises and everyone goes haw haw haw like he's being really funny.

I just bounced a bit higher on my trampoline and took no notice. And that was great! I was way up, out of reach. I didn't even blush! The only problem was that I stayed up there for double maths. Mr Trimble's comments were rather what I would call *cutting*. Rather uncalled for. Well, anyway I think so. I mean, love is one of life's key experiences. Love has inspired some of man's greatest creations. (And women's, too, of course.) It should not be sneered at.

But this grain brain, Kevin Mutimer, who is one of the Bonehead's mates (Rosa calls him the Mutant. She's got a name for everybody!) yells out, 'He can't help being half-witted, he's in love!'

At which the whole class brays and sniggers, and Mr Trimble, who I should say is old and decrepit and has this ancient crumpled neck and a head like a thousand-year-old tortoise and has probably never experienced love, or if he has he's forgotten about it, he curls his lip and goes, 'A most regrettable state of affairs, to be sure! Guaranteed to cause premature brain death. No excuse, however, for not paying attention in my maths class!' And he goes and gives me a hundred lines.

Lines. I ask you. But Mr Trimble is out of the ark. He used to whack people with a ruler until someone threatened to take him to the European Court. Rosa reckons the entire school should be taken there. She says it's full of bigots, blimps and boneheads. She is often rather extreme in her views, but in this case I think she is probably right.

Noah laughed when I told him. About the lines, I mean.

'Serve you right! You Year Eights are a load of yobs.'

'I'm not a yob,' I said. I resented that! Being tarred with the same brush as Bonehead and the Mutant.

'So what did you do? You must have done

something to upset the old boy.'

'I had a momentary lapse of concentration,' I said.

'You mean you weren't paying attention!'

'My mind,' I said, 'was otherwise engaged.' I wasn't telling him what it was otherwise engaged on! That was personal; and me and Noah didn't discuss things that were personal. At least, I didn't think we did. It kind of threw me when he gave this broad grin and said, 'Daydreaming about your beloved?'

I can't properly remember what I said in reply, but it was probably something like, 'Whatdoyou whodoyouwhatareyouwhy?' In other words, just a meaningless babble. I was pretty embarrassed, to tell you the truth.

'It's nothing to be ashamed of,' said Noah. 'You don't have to go all bashful on me!'

Next thing I'm, like, totally gobsmacked* as he leans back against the door – us being in my bedroom at the time – and all casual goes, 'You're not the only one. It's great, isn't it? Being in love!'

It's weird, really, and I can't even begin to explain it, but that made me even more embarrassed than I already was. I mean, Noah – talking to *me* – about love!

* Rosa says this is a stupid and vulgar expression to use in a book and why can't I simply say I was amazed? OK! I was amazed. To put it mildly.

I thought at first that maybe he was only joking, but I could tell that he wasn't. He was serious! He was obviously feeling pretty excited, which I guess is why he needed to talk about it. 'Cos as far as I knew he'd never experienced love before. Mum used to accuse him of playing fast and loose with girls' affections.

'You pick them up, you put them down...what do you think they are? *Objects?*'

Now, suddenly, he was smitten. At the age of almost seventeen! I guess it hits you harder when you start so late in life.

We didn't exactly settle down for a cosy chat. I mean, cosy chats are not what we're into. We mainly talked about Mr Trimble, as a matter of fact. Noah said how his hormones had probably withered and died some time back at the turn of the last century, and we got a bit of banter going about how he might have been when he was young and frolicsome.

'A gruesome thought!' said Noah.

I think we both felt safer, talking about Mr Trimble. At any rate, it stopped me being embarrassed.

By the time we'd done Mr-Trimble-discovering-his-hormones, and Mr-Trimble-chasing-wenches, and Mr-Trimble's-first-kiss, I was feeling bold enough to ask Noah the ten thousand dollar question.

'So who is it?' I said.

He wouldn't tell.

'You think I want the piss taken out of me?'

'I wouldn't, I wouldn't!'

'You might not. But look what happened at Christmas!'

Christmas had been pretty dire.

'But no one would know,' I said. 'I wouldn't tell them! I wouldn't tell anyone!'

'You must be joking!' said Noah. 'You'd be off round to Rosa's just as fast as your legs could carry you!'

It was true, I couldn't promise not to tell Rosa because me and Rosa tell each other everything. Pretty well.

'But Rosa wouldn't tell!' I said. 'I'd swear her to secrecy!'

He still wouldn't say. I grumbled about it. I said, 'It's not fair! You know about me and her.'

Noah said, 'That's the way the cookie crumbles, kiddo! In any case, I can hardly help knowing about you and Rosa. The whole world knows about you and Rosa! You, my little brother—' he pressed a finger against my nose, '—ought to take a leaf out of my book and learn a bit of discretion...you won't catch me making a spectacle of myself in public!'

Needless to say, me and Rosa chewed it over. We discussed it from every angle. Rosa is like Mum: she really thrives on gossip! She says that it is simply taking a normal human interest in people.

'Men are into *things*. Women are into *people*.'

She wanted me to tell her exactly what Noah had said. She wanted to sift through it and see if she could dredge up any clues. But she couldn't! He hadn't dropped so much as a hint.

'It's got to be someone he's met recently.'

'Down the Sports Club, maybe?'

Noah was at the Sports Club two or three nights a week, plus every weekend. Mum and Dad had given him a year's subscription for his birthday. They'd asked me if I'd like to join as well, and I'd discussed it with Rosa (since we only do things together) but we'd decided we weren't really into that sort of thing. Swimming and tennis and all that. Working out. Getting up a sweat. But Noah was, so we reckoned anyone he fell for would have to share the same interest.

'It can't be Emily,' said Rosa. 'She's a couch potato.'

I said, 'What's a couch potato?'

'Someone that doesn't like exercise,' said Rosa.

'You mean, like us?'

'Not like us! We go for walks.'

I suppose that counts as exercise, though I'm not sure that Noah would think so. And we don't even do that all that often. Mostly we just hunch over a chessboard. We have become couch vegetables!

'I wonder,' said Rosa, 'if we ought to join the Sports Club after all? It's the only way we're ever likely to find out!'

I don't know whether she was serious or not. Being Rosa, she could well have been. She'll go to any lengths to uncover a secret. She's good at it, too! Detective work, picking up clues. But she didn't get anywhere with Noah. In the end she grew so desperate she actually asked him outright.

'*Please* won't you tell us who your girlfriend is?'

'Wouldn't you like to know?' said Noah.

'Well, I would,' agreed Rosa, ''cos it's keeping me awake at night.'

'Really?' said Noah. 'I had no idea!'

'He's not going to tell,' I said.

'No, he's not,' said Noah. 'Some of us like to conduct our love life in private!'

'Love life,' moaned Rosa, when we were on our own. 'He's got a love life and we don't know who it is! Oh, this is too gross! We've just got to find out!'

Rosa became, like, obsessed. All our conversations started to revolve around Noah and his love life. Who was this mystery person? Who could it be? Where had he met them?

Rosa ran through every girl she could think of, and when she ran out of real girls she dreamt up pretend ones.

'She's got to be pretty! He'd never go for anyone plain.'

'Why not?' I said. I thought she was being somewhat sexist here. 'Why wouldn't he go for someone plain? If she was, like, good at tennis or something?'

'*Because*,' said Rosa. 'Good-looking people always choose other good-looking people. It's one of the rules.'

'What about when young girls go and get married to disgusting old wrinklies?' I said.

'That's different,' said Rosa. 'They're just doing

it for the money, or because they're looking for a father figure, or security, or something. Believe me! Watch my lips...whoever it is, they are going to be beeeeeeeeautiful. It's got to be someone down the Club! Plays tennis like crazy. That's how they met! Playing mixed doubles. She's very tall and very slim and...very athletic and...*golden.*'

I said, 'Golden?'

'Golden,' said Rosa. 'Absolutely! She spent the Christmas holidays in a ski resort.'

'So her family must be quite well off,' I said.

'Obviously, or she couldn't belong to the Sports Club.'

'What's her name?'

'Mm...' Rosa crinkled her nose, which is this thing that she does when she's concentrating. 'Something classy. Emma, or Sarah, or... Parthenope! Parthenope Blenkinsop-Smythe.'

I objected to that. 'Noah wouldn't fall for someone called Blenkinsop-Smythe! That's disgusting, that is!'

Rosa agreed that perhaps it was a bit over the top.

'She's probably just called Jo, or Alice, or something. But she's still golden!'

We played the game for a day or two, and then

something happened which made me lose all interest in Noah and who his girlfriend might be. I got home from school one afternoon and Mum was on the phone. This is not unusual! Mum is often on the phone. In fact she's more often on it than off. Our phone bill is positively enormous; Dad is always complaining about it.

I think before I go any further I would like to say, right here and now, that I was not eavesdropping. There was no reason that I should. I mean, Mum's telephone conversations go on for ever and are pretty dead boring. However, it just so happened that I was on my way down the hall and I heard her voice.

I heard her say, 'Sweetheart, don't worry! It'll be quite safe, I promise you. There'll be no one else here…just you and me. All right? Trust me! I'll see you as arranged.'

And then she put the phone down, and I stood in the hall all trembly and dithering, with a million questions zizzing round my brain. First and foremost: what was going to happen to me if Mum and Dad broke up???

Pathetic, really, but I am trying to tell the truth here.

The other big one was, *who*? Plus why, and

where, and when. Not to mention for what purpose. But mainly, who.

I guess the simplest thing would have been to ask.

'Er...Mum! Who were you talking to?'

But it's not like it was something I would normally do. I mean, you don't as a rule question your mum about her telephone calls. Besides, it didn't occur to me. Instead, I waited till Mum had gone upstairs, then I nipped in and pressed one-four-seven-one, gambling that whoever it was might have called Mum, rather than Mum calling them. And they had! And the number was local. And I did this really sneaky thing that I don't think, probably, I ought to have done, but I did it anyway. I used the code that lets you make phone calls without the person at the other end knowing where you're calling from (unless you're being obscene, in which case the police can always trace you, at least I think they can). I dialled the number that Mum had been talking to and the person at the other end picked up the receiver and said, 'Hallo,' and it was Lars Kennedy. I recognised his voice immediately. It was very distinctive.

I didn't speak to him. I just banged the receiver

down. And after that it wasn't my brother's love life I was bothered about, it was my mum's.

chapter
six

I tell most everything to Rosa. Pretty much. I wasn't being disloyal to Mum! It was just that I really needed to talk. Maybe you might think the obvious person would have been Noah, him being my brother and all, and especially after the conversation we'd had the other day. But although I was pretty flattered that he'd confided in me – I mean, it gave me a really good feeling, being close to him like that – at the same time it had definitely embarrassed me. I couldn't talk to Noah about Mum! And needless to say, I could hardly talk to Dad. So I talked to Rosa.

Rosa agreed that it looked bad. She agreed it looked as though Mum and Lars Kennedy really were having an affair, but she pointed out that my mum and dad are very sophisticated people. She said they could probably 'handle a little adultery'.

'They may even have an agreement about it…you know? You do your thing, I'll do mine.'

In fact, she said, that was most probably what they did have.

'Your mum's obviously not too bothered about your dad finding out. She'd be more careful, otherwise. I expect he's doing exactly the same sort of thing! Only he's probably doing it with his secretary, or someone. It seems to me,' said Rosa, 'that one has to be realistic. Having affairs is what grown-ups do. I mean, grown-ups like your mum and dad. Celebs, and that. Not mine, so much. They're more stick-in-the-mud. But really, I don't think you ought to worry about it. It simply means that they have a mature relationship. I mean, they still get on all right, don't they? They're still friends?'

I thought about it, and had to agree that they were. Mum occasionally pulls Dad's leg – about his autographs, for example – and she does tend to flirt with other men, like the milkman and the window cleaner and even the guy that comes to unblock the drains, but that's just Mum. She does it without even thinking; it's like second nature. Dad doesn't seem to mind. And if ever he's seriously down, like for example when he most desperately wanted to get this daytime radio slot and they went and gave it to a person that is a total nerd (according to Dad), Mum is always sympathetic. She's always loyal, she always sticks up for him. So I reckon they really do love each other, but it's like Rosa says, they have this *mature relationship.*

I felt a bit better after talking things over. I still didn't like the idea – of Mum and Lars Kennedy, I mean; but as Rosa said, you have to be realistic. So I tried to stop worrying, though I couldn't help it always being there, at the back of my mind. I have to tell you, it's kind of creepy, believing that your mum – *your mum* – is jumping into bed with someone that's not your dad. Especially when that someone happens to go to your school and be only a few years older than you are.

I'd worked out in my mind that the only time Mum could absolutely one hundred per cent guarantee she'd be alone in the house was Wednesday afternoon, when I was at school, and Noah was playing rugger, and Dad was at the studio. He always goes in early on a Wednesday to record things. There wasn't any way I could discover whether Lars Kennedy was free at that time, but in Upper School you have loads of free periods so it would be easy enough for him to bunk off.

When I got home on Wednesday, I felt like a tracker dog, going round the house. I just had this feeling that I'd sense if Lars had been there.

Mum asked me what the problem was.

'Are you on a pilgrimage, or something?'

I said, 'What?'

'What,' mimicked Mum, pulling this halfwit face. She was really playing it cool. 'You're in constant motion. Just keep still! What's the matter? Are you looking for something?'

Signs of Lars Kennedy. But I wasn't brave enough to say that to Mum. Instead, later on, I asked Noah.

'Do people ever have Wednesday afternoon off?'

'What are you talking about?' said Noah.

'If you're not playing a match. Do you ever have Wednesday afternoon off?'

'Possibly. Sometimes. Why?'

'Just wondered,' I mumbled. I wasn't even brave enough to ask Noah. If I did, I would have to admit that I was spying on Mum, and I didn't want to admit that even to myself.

Next day was Thursday, the Day of Difference

day. I don't think any of us were mad excited by it. We'd been told at the beginning of term who the speaker was going to be, and it wasn't anyone to get lit up about. Just some woman that had written a book that had won a load of prizes. *Children's* prizes. It was a book written for kids!

'Teenagers, actually,' said Noah, when I taxed him with it.

'I thought you said it was someone that would give us a rough time!'

'She will. Believe me…she will!'

'How do you know?' I said.

'I know someone who's heard her speak. She'll take you lot to the cleaners!'

I didn't believe him; none of us did. A kids' writer! And a woman, at that. We reckoned we'd been short-changed. We wanted a holocaust survivor! We wanted a paraplegic that climbed mountains! We didn't want some woman that wrote kids' books. It was belittling. That was what the Mutant said, and for once I agreed with him. Definitely belittling.

By the time we were herded into the library on Thursday morning, we were feeling pretty stroppy. This woman was sitting there with Ms King, our librarian. Hannah Douglas, her name was. She didn't look too bad. She wasn't young, but I didn't hold that against her. I mean, I try not to be ageist. And she was quite presentable. Small and tough-looking and wearing jeans. Jeans were cool! I like women in jeans. (Unless they have big bums. I don't go for bums! Bonehead does. He describes himself as a bottoms man. He would!)

Anyway, this woman, Hannah Douglas, she starts in straightaway telling us about this book she's written. The one that's won all the prizes. It's about someone that's gay and what happens when he comes out. How his mum starts crying and his dad won't speak to him and his sister's the only one that doesn't give him the elbow. In the end, after everyone's been beastly to him, he goes off to uni and meets up with other guys that are gay and everything ends happily.

'That is,' says Hannah (she tells us to call her Hannah) 'as happily as can be expected in a world that is less than tolerant.'

We're sitting there listening to all this in a kind of glum silence. Or perhaps not so much glum as...resentful. That's the word. We're *resentful*. We're not actually showing it, partly because our form master, Mr Hussey, is sitting there with his arms folded and his eyes zapping about like lasers, and he'd be vitriolic as hell if anyone dared to so much as roll his eyes; but partly, also, because it's one of the quaint old redneck traditions of Hadley that you have to be polite to guests.* But we're less than enchanted. And I still can't see why Noah reckoned this woman would give us a rough time. I mean, all she is is a *kids'* writer, for heaven's sake! We're Year Eight. It's an insult, really.

And then it's like she's reading our minds because she says that after talking to us she's going to go and talk to the Upper School. Like, 'If I'm good enough for them, I should be good enough for you.' Noah hadn't told me this. What's she going to talk to them about?

'We're going to have a discussion,' she says. 'Which is what I hope I'm going to have with you.'

And she brings out this sheaf of papers and starts dishing them out, up and down the rows. I wondered why we'd all been sat at tables: this explains it. She's prepared a questionnaire, which we all have to fill in.

'Don't be afraid to tell the truth,' she says. 'This is strictly anonymous! No one will know what you've answered.'

Which is just as well, as the questions she's asking are really squirm-making. Like, for

---

* Rosa says that sarcasm is the lowest form of wit. *So what?*

instance, 'Are you prejudiced against people that are gay?' 'How would you feel if your best friend suddenly came out?' Etc. and so forth.

I could see old Bonehead and the Mutant pulling faces at each other. What was going on here??? An invasion of privacy, if you asked me. I mean, I know it was anonymous and all, but I didn't see that this woman had any right to be asking us this sort of thing. Some of these questions were quite personal.

One or two people were shooting anxious glances at Mr Hussey. Do we really have to do this? But Mr Hussey just shrugged his shoulders like it was no concern of his.

'You've been told what to do. Get on with it!'

I suppose it was pretty stupid, really, trying to disguise my handwriting, but I bet I wasn't the only one that did. I had this vision of Mr Hussey going through the papers afterwards and checking who'd put what.

Of course I knew what the point of it all was. The point of it was to show how open-minded we were. We were supposed to be open-minded: that's what the Day of Difference was all about. But she'd said to be truthful, so that's what I was.

Like where it said are you prejudiced, I said

'Yes', and where it said 'How would you feel about your best friend coming out?' I put 'Shaken'. I was going to put 'Disgusted' but I stopped to think about it and it made me sound like one of those really geeky guys that sometimes ring Dad. ('Disgusted from Droitwich' is what Dad calls them. I don't know what he's got against Droitwich.) Anyway, I didn't want to be like them so I put shaken, instead.

I *would* have been shaken. My best friend was Tom Bacon that left at the end of Year Seven to go to boarding school. We were really close. We'd even slept together in a tent in his back garden! I wouldn't like to think I'd shared a tent with anyone that was gay.

Later on, where she said about two guys kissing each other (I told you it was squirm-making) I put SICK and underlined it three times.

I couldn't help it! The thought of guys kissing each other just turned my stomach. There wasn't any point saying it didn't when it did. Least, that's how it seemed to me.

I was being truthful; right?

When everyone's finished, she gathers up all the papers and talks her way through them, so that we can discover how bigoted and narrow-minded we are. Which we are. Just three out of eighteen claim they're not prejudiced, and wouldn't mind, wouldn't feel sick, wouldn't be turned up, etc., and I bet they're only saying it to score brownie points. 'Cos they know that's what they're meant to say, showing how unprejudiced they are. We're all looking round, wondering who it is, but Hannah's not giving anything away.

'Well,' she said, 'this is much as I expected. It's one of the reasons I wrote the book! To challenge people's prejudices...try and change their perceptions. Let's start the ball rolling! Someone tell me *why* they're so prejudiced.'

There's a pause here. No one wants to be first! Then old Bonehead shoots up his hand and goes, 'Because it's not natural, if you want to know.'

'Not natural in what sense?' says Hannah.

Well, says Bonehead, most people aren't like it.

If they were, adds the Mutant, the world would be depopulated.

Someone says, 'And a good thing, too!' and for a moment we get a bit sidetracked, but then Hannah pulls it back again by agreeing with Bonehead.

'Most people aren't like it. True! But what is that to the point?'

Bonehead stares at her, his eyes popping. The point is self-evident! Isn't it?

'Most people aren't blind,' says Hannah.

Is Bonehead prejudiced against blind people?

Bonehead blusters a bit but can only think to say, 'That's different!' Whereupon Hannah asks him how it's different, thus stumping him for an answer, and the Mutant has to come to his aid. Blind people, he tells us, don't interfere with young kids.

A boy called Cosmo Bailey adds that they don't corrupt others; and Bonehead, regaining confidence, says that in any case people can't help being blind.

Someone then suggests that gay people can't help being gay.

'It's just the way they're born.'

'They don't have to go round corrupting people,' says Cosmo.

'Or interfering with kids,' agrees the Mutant.

There's a bit of dissent here. A somewhat nerdy boy called Simon Oliphant protests that most gay people don't interfere with kids.

'*Or* corrupt.'

I thought that was quite brave of him, actually. It was what I'd been thinking, only I couldn't quite bring myself to say it. I didn't want any part of this discussion, if I'm to be honest.

After a bit, Hannah says that we don't really seem to be getting anywhere. She says, 'I feel that you're all stepping too carefully…you're trying too hard to be polite! It's holding you back. Forget good manners! Let's have a bit of verbal rough-and-tumble. Don't worry, I can take it! And you won't get into trouble, I give you my word.' She looks at Mr Hussey, who gives this sickly smile. 'Come on! Let's hear from you.'

So Cosmo, getting bold, asks her how come she's written a book about a teenage boy when she's never been a teenage boy.

'I mean, what do you *know* about teenage boys?'

A good question! But Hannah takes it on the chin. She says that she's a writer and that it's a writer's job to use their imagination.

'But you could have got it all wrong,' says Cosmo.

Hannah agrees that she could have.

'But without reading the book you wouldn't know, would you?' she says.

Noah's right: she can give as good as she gets!

Bonehead, trying to do to Hannah what he does to me when he calls me Joly, asks her if she herself is gay. She's not fazed! Not one little bit. She doesn't even blush. She says quite calmly that she's not, but that it's a valid question.

'Have you ever had a sex change?' asks the Mutant, and I can see Mr Hussey beetling at him from under his brows. He can't tell him off because Hannah's given her word, but he'd like to!

'No,' says Hannah, not batting an eyelid. 'No sex change. Sorry to disappoint you!'

My friend Mark Jarman, who I'd sort of taken to hanging out with after Tom had left, and who has a bit more brain than Bonehead or the Mutant, asks her what exactly she is trying to get us to say.

'Are you trying to get us to say there's nothing wrong with being gay?'

Hannah denies it. She says, 'I'm not trying to get you to say anything. I'm simply trying to get you to examine your prejudices. But if you're asking whether I *personally* am saying there's nothing wrong with being gay...then the answer is yes. That is what I'm saying.'

Someone, somewhere, gives an angry hiss of disapproval. Hannah carries on, regardless.

'I'm not only saying there's nothing wrong with it, I'm saying there's nothing abnormal about it. It means you're a bit different from the majority, perhaps; but so what? Wasn't Beethoven?'

Some goon at the back cries, 'Beethoven was *gay?*'

'Who cares about Beethoven anyway?' says Bonehead. Actually, I'm surprised he's even heard of him.

'All right,' says Hannah. 'Forget about Beethoven. How about…Alan Porter?'

She doesn't really say Alan Porter. Alan Porter is just a name I made up. The name she actually says is the name of someone pretty famous that I can't mention as I don't want to be sued. I mean, there isn't any reason he *should* sue me, not as far as I can tell, except maybe he wouldn't like to think of his name being bandied about in a discussion about gays. I just don't want to run any risks, is all.

'Alan Porter's not a poof!' yells the Mutant.

'I didn't say he was,' says Hannah. 'I said he was *different.* How many people could kick a ball the way he does? It's almost uncanny! But the world needs people who are different. Difference should be celebrated. It's nothing to be ashamed of. It would be a very dull place if we were all the same!'

At the end of the session she asks how many of

us still feel as we did at the beginning. She gets us to write it down on a piece of paper. I kind of waver, but in the end I have to put yes; I still feel the same. I mean, if I am being honest. She hasn't said anything to change my mind. Not really.

The result is 14 to 4. Only one person has gone over to her side! You'd think she'd be disappointed, but in fact she doesn't seem too upset.

'I haven't exactly won over your hearts and minds,' she says, 'but hopefully I've given you something to think about. Which is, after all, the object of the exercise!'

Me and Mark talked it over during the break. We didn't ask each other how we'd finally voted; that would have been too personal. I was still grumbling about being palmed off with a kids' writer. I'd kind of latched on to this as my main peeve.

'I dunno. She was pretty good,' said Mark.

'Yeah, but a *kids'* writer!'

Mark said that according to Mr Pelham (Mr Pelham being the one that had invited her) this book that she'd written, *Love Lies Bleeding*, was worth having a look at.

'What, with a title like that?'

''Cording to Mr Pelham. He said after we'd heard her talk, we all ought to go and get it out the school library.'

'Why *after*? 'Cos he didn't want to put us off!'

'No, he said she wasn't here to talk about the book, not particularly. She was here to talk about the issue.'

I said in that case it might have been more to the point if he'd got someone that was actually gay. Mark, however, said he didn't think he would have dared to do that. He said Clause 28 didn't allow it.

'So you mean, like, he had to slip it in through the back door kind of thing?' I said.

I wasn't being vulgar when I said this. I mean, it wasn't meant as a *double entendre*, or anything smutty. But the minute I'd said it, I saw that it was. Well, given what we'd been talking about. Mark saw it, too. It made us a bit silly and crude. But it was only the two of us! What I'm saying is, I don't think it was harmful. Not really.

I discussed it with Rosa later on. The visit, and the questionnaire, and the final vote, and everything. I admitted to her that I was prejudiced. Rosa said, 'What's to be prejudiced about? I don't understand!'

I said, 'That's because you're a girl.'

'Sexist rubbish!' said Rosa. 'It wouldn't bother me one little bit if Sian came out and said she was gay.'

Sian is her best friend at school.

'After all, what different would it make? She'd still be the same person.'

'She wouldn't be the person you'd thought she was.'

'So what?'

I said, 'You'd always be wondering if she fancied you.'

'Think I'd care?' retorted Rosa.

There are times when Rosa is impossible.

'Look, just tell me! What does it actually *matter*?' she said. 'Really and truly? When it comes down to it? It's not hurting you! It's not hurting anyone. It's not like being an arms manufacturer, or something. I don't see what all the fuss is about! You haven't given me one rational argument. Just that it makes you want to throw up.'

'Isn't that enough?' I said.

She looked at me, reproachfully. 'You know it isn't!'

'Well, anyway,' I said, and I probably said it a bit

sullenly, like you do when you feel you're under attack, 'it's promoting homosexuality and that's against the law. You're not supposed to do that! There's going to be trouble about it!'

Rosa narrowed her eyes. 'What do you mean?'

'Someone's going to get chewed out.' There was a rumour that Fanny hadn't known about Hannah; that Mr Pelham had gone and arranged the visit without consulting him. 'Some people are pretty mad, I can tell you!'

'What people?'

'Ben Arrowhead, for one.'

'That Bonehead!'

'He's going to complain to his parents. He doesn't reckon it's right, someone coming in and telling us all to be gay.'

'She didn't tell you all to be gay! She just said there's nothing wrong with it.'

'Well, she oughtn't to have done. You're not allowed to say things like that!'

'Oh, for goodness' sake!' cried Rosa.

I don't like it when Rosa holds me in contempt; it upsets me quite a lot. I mean, I really value her opinion. But sometimes there are these feelings that you have and no amount of intellectual argument will make them go away or change them into other kinds of feelings.

Rosa is very clever, but there are some things she just doesn't understand.

chapter seven

Next day, the news was all over school. Cosmo Bailey had got it from his cousin, who had got it from his brother, who was in the sixth form. Cosmo had instantly rung Bonehead, who had rung the Mutant, who was now excitedly rushing round, Friday morning, telling all the rest of us.

'Have you heard?'

'Heard what?'

'Lars Kennedy! He's come out!'

'*What?*'

'Lars Kennedy?'

'Come out?'

'You're joking!'

But he wasn't; it was true. Lars Kennedy had come out, and it was all the fault of Hannah Douglas.

'My dad,' said Bonehead, stiff with virtue, 'is

coming in to see Fanny about it. He's made an appointment. He says he's not going to let the matter rest, he wants a thorough investigation.'

What had happened, according to the Mutant (according to Bonehead, according to Cosmo's cousin's brother) was that Hannah had had the same discussion with the Upper School as she'd had with us, as a result of which Lars Kennedy had felt moved to stand up and inform everyone that he was gay.

My immediate reaction – well, after the first burst of shock horror *wow*! – was to feel relieved. Because if Lars Kennedy was gay, he obviously couldn't have been doing what I thought he was doing with my mum, so that was one big worry out the way. Actually, it was *the* big worry out the way. I didn't have any others. It didn't matter to me if the guy was gay. I was a bit taken aback – I mean, it's not what you expect, and it wasn't like he'd been obvious about it. Well, it didn't seem to me that he had, though there were a few clever clogs, notably Cosmo Bailey and Bonehead, who insisted it came as no surprise to *them*.

'Spot these things a mile off.'

'Guy's a screaming poof! Only got to look at him.'

'Brown hatter.'

'Bender.'

'Bum bandit.'

Etc.

I then remembered how I'd once complained to Rosa that Lars was creepy, skulking about in the bushes. So I *had* known! I'd known all along. I just hadn't realised.

I might as well admit, that made me feel somewhat pleased with myself. Cosmo and Bonehead weren't the only ones who could spot these things a mile off. I could, too!

I immediately told everyone about it. Eyes widened; breaths were sucked in. Heady stuff! Joel Bradbeer had *practically caught him at it.*

The kudos was quite gratifying. But even at the time, I knew it wasn't something I could admit to Rosa. I think there was a part of me, even then, that acknowledged it as unworthy. Lars had laid himself wide open, and I was right there, sticking the boot in along with all the rest.

The general consensus was that Lars must be some kind of an idiot. Bad enough being that way in the first place, but why go shooting his mouth off about it?

'It's what they do,' said Bonehead. Bonehead seemed to have set himself up as some kind of an expert on the subject. What he didn't know about poofs wasn't worth knowing. 'All up front and in your face.' He smacked his lips, suggestively. 'Screamers, the lot of 'em!'

If anyone was sympathetic, they weren't saying; not even Simon Oliphant, that I thought might have been. He'd held out against the notion of gays interfering with kids, but he wasn't going out on a limb for Lars Kennedy. Nobody was.

'Guy must have a screw loose.'

'Must have a *screw*!'

Har har har.

'Yeah, but it was that woman pushed him into it. She oughtn't to have been here!'

I bumped into Lars later that day, on my way to the library. He nodded and said, 'Hi,' no different from how he always was. I wondered how he had the nerve. I mean, just walking around the place the same as usual, with everyone knowing about him. I wouldn't! I'd sooner die than have people know I was gay. If I *was* gay, which I'm not. But if I was.

That is, actually, what I thought. That I would sooner die. I didn't really mean it, I don't think. But if I'd been gay and going to our school I'd never have let on in a million years.

I met up with Noah on the way home. Sometimes Mum used to pick us up in the car, but otherwise we caught the bus, though not very often the same one. There's one at 3.45 and one an hour later. Today we both got the 3.45. We didn't sit together because I was with Cosmo and Mark Jarman. Cosmo was still going on about Lars. I know I've said about how Mum and Rosa enjoy a gossip, like it's just a woman's thing, but I have to admit, we'd given the Lars Kennedy story a pretty good going over, the whole lot of us. Me included. I guess it was quite a big thing in our normally uneventful lives.

'I mean, who'd want to get in a shower with it?' shouted Cosmo. 'Who'd w—'

'You don't have to bawl,' said Mark.

'I'm not bawling!' bawled Cosmo. And then he caught sight of Noah, a few seats away, and lowered his voice. 'Hey, Joly! Your brother's in Upper School. What's he have to say about it?'

'Dunno,' I said.

So far, Noah hadn't said anything at all. He'd never even mentioned about Lars coming out; he hadn't even asked how we'd got on with Hannah. But Noah's never been a gossip merchant.

I tried to think of a way to bring the subject up as we walked from the bus together. The best I could do was, 'Everyone's talking about what happened yesterday.'

'So I heard,' said Noah. 'Loud voice your friend's got.'

I said, 'He's not my friend. He just happens to be in my class.'

'Glad to hear it.'

'We all reckon that woman was to blame...old Hannah wotsername.'

'Really.'

'Yeah, well, I mean, it's against the law, that kind of thing.'

'What kind of thing?'

'Encouraging people.'

'To do what?'

'Think it's OK to be gay.'

'Which it isn't?'

'No! Well – what I mean, people can't *help* it, necessarily. I'm not saying they can help it. But it's still against the law. Encouraging them.'

'I see.'

'Well, it is!' I said.

'So there you go,' said Noah.

'She's going to get into trouble,' I said. 'Her or Mr Pelham. One of 'em!'

Noah stayed silent.

'Someone's got to. Coming into school and carrying on like that!'

'Vindictive little creep, aren't you?' said Noah.

I flushed. I didn't like that! I'd thought Noah would be on my side.

'I don't reckon it's right,' I mumbled. 'You couldn't come into a school and encourage people to be racist.'

'Oh, for God's sake,' said Noah. 'Don't be so pathetic!'

That's all he would say; after that he just clammed up on me. He got quite snotty when I tried to push him. He used language which I am certainly not going to repeat in a book. I mean, on an obscenity rating it would get at least five stars. Quite unusual, actually; Noah's not one of those people that swears for the sake of swearing. I reckoned what it was, old Hannah had got to him. She'd made him ashamed. So now he was too scared to say what he really thought. That was the danger of these sort of people; that's what they did. They perverted young minds. They had to be stopped!

For once, I was in complete agreement with Bonehead. His dad *ought* to go to Fanny. If Lars Kennedy got the piss taken out of him, it would be all Hannah's fault.

Anyway, that was the way I saw it.

It seemed to be the way Mum and Dad saw it, as well. Mum, at any rate. She'd already heard the story, and I wondered how, until she explained and all became clear.

'Lars rang me yesterday, after he'd done it. He came to see me, you know. Just this week. W—'

'He came to see you?' It was obviously news to Noah. Not to me, of course, 'cos I'd been spying. '*Lars*? Came to see *you*?'

'He needed someone to talk to. He knows I'm an agony aunt. We had a long session, he did a lot of soul searching, h—'

'About what?' said Noah. He sounded a bit nervous, like he didn't like the idea of Lars coming in on his own to speak to Mum. I wasn't sure that I did, either.

'You don't have to be all suspicious!' said Mum. 'We simply discussed whether or not he ought to come out.'

'And what did you say?' Dad looked at Mum, curiously. She hadn't even told him!

'I advised him to think very carefully. I gave him a couple of numbers to ring – told him to have a chat with them before coming to any decision. Then this woman, this – Douglas, or whatever her name is, came waltzing in, and I guess the whole thing just blew up.'

'Did anyone suspect?' Dad turned to Noah. Noah shrugged. 'I mean, it wasn't that obvious, was it? Or was it?'

'Not to me,' said Mum. 'I'd have said he was very discreet.'

'Silly young fool! He should have kept it that way. What on earth possessed him? At some schools, maybe; he might get away with it. But Hadley? It's not exactly noted for its artistic sensibilities!'

'So why did you send us there?' said Noah. And I thought I heard a note of bitterness in his voice, which was odd, since I'd always reckoned Noah was made for Hadley.

'We didn't do it lightly, I can assure you,' said Dad. 'We thought about it long and hard. In the end it just seemed...right.'

'Why?'

'Well—' Dad waved a hand. 'Good reputation. Sports facilities. Small classes.'

'That's all?'

'It's enough, isn't it?'

'Don't you like it there?' I said.

Nobody took any notice of me.

'We gave it very careful consideration,' said Mum.

'What's wrong with it?' I said. I was really curious. I mean, I know what Rosa thinks, but Noah was like some kind of hero. He was popular, he was one of the leading lights. 'What don't you like about it?'

'Everything!' snapped Noah.

'*Everything?*'

Pleadingly, Mum said, 'We thought it would give you a bit of polish.'

Noah's lip curled. 'You mean, like we're pieces of furniture?'

'Look, whatever you think,' said Mum, 'going to a school like Hadley does give you advantages. Let's be honest about it! Why are you all of a sudden attacking us? We did what we thought was best. We thought we were giving you a chance in life. I know the place is a bit...gung-ho. A bit blokeish. But there are lots of good things about it!'

'Unless, of course, you happen to be gay,' said Dad. 'And go shouting it from the rooftops. Why couldn't he just keep stumm? He'll be lucky to survive!'

Noah muttered something under his breath.

'What?' said Dad. 'What was that?'

'I said, that's right, blame the victim,' said Noah.

'I'm not blaming him! But he has rather brought it on himself. You've got to admit, it was pretty dumb.'

'Oh, come on!' said Mum. 'He's young, he's idealistic.'

'Idealistic?' Dad snorted. 'Is that what you call it? Getting up in front of a load of young thugs and boasting that you're gay? I call it asking for trouble!'

'Well, maybe it was, but I don't think you can accuse him of boasting. That wasn't at all how he saw it. He saw it more as making a statement. Standing up and being counted. You have to hand it to him,' said Mum. 'It was a brave thing to do!'

'Foolhardy,' said Dad. 'How are the young thugs taking it?'

The question was addressed to Noah, but Noah just humped a shoulder.

'I suppose they're all being desperately macho?'

'Bonehead is,' I said.

'He's in for a rough ride, whichever way you look at it.'

'Poor lad!' Mum still had a soft spot for Lars, you could tell. When I say still, what I mean is, it must have been a big disappointment to her. Fancying him like she did. Or maybe not. Women are odd like that. They don't seem to react the same way as men.

'Maybe,' said Mum, 'we should invite him over.'

'What for?' That was Noah, practically jumping down her throat. Mum looked at him, reproachfully.

'I thought it would be rather nice if we asked him for a meal.'

'Why?'

'Well, for God's sake! Why not?'

'He wouldn't want to.'

'*He* wouldn't? Or you wouldn't? Don't tell me you're one of the macho brigade!'

Earnestly, trying to help, I said to Mum, 'It's not being macho, but you wouldn't want to be in a shower with him'

Mum gave a short yelp of distinctly unamused laughter.

'Oh, my Lord! Hark at it. Joel, just listen to yourself!'

I felt my cheeks go red.

'Leave him alone,' said Noah. 'Just leave the whole thing alone. Just drop it! Stop patronising people.'

We watched in amazement as Noah shoved back his chair and went slamming out of the room.

Noah's not the sort of person to go slamming out of places. He's usually pretty cool and laid-back.

Fretfully, Mum said, 'What does he mean, patronising?'

'I think what he means,' said Dad, 'is that he'd rather we didn't go poking our noses in. If word got about that Lars had been round here—'

'What?' said Mum, in a rather tight sort of voice.

'It might not do his image any good.'

'You mean, he *is* one of the macho brigade!'

'No! He's just a normal regular teenage lad who like any other teenage lad is highly sensitive about such things. Don't go getting on his case! It's not like he's turning his back on a friend. They were hardly bosom pals, as I understand it.'

'No, they weren't,' I said.

'Oh, well! That's all right, then.' Mum began snatching up used cutlery. She did it in a somewhat frenzied fashion. 'That's a great weight off my mind! We can all stop worrying.'

Me and Dad looked at each other. Dad pulled a face.

'Now we're in the dog house,' he said.

'Well, really! The pair of you.' Mum clattered

plates on to the tray, with a quite unnecessary amount of noise. 'You're like two old mastodons!'

I looked that word up in the dictionary. It means a genus of extinct elephant. I resented my mum calling me an extinct elephant. Seemed to me it was me and Dad and Noah getting all the flak while Lars was being treated like some kind of hero. Seemed to me that wasn't right.

You understand, I'm telling it like it was. I have to write what it was really like; not how I wish it had been.

Just two old mastodons. I guess Mum was right.

chapter eight

When we got in to school on Monday, we found that someone had sprayed graffiti right across the bog wall:

LARS KENNEDY IS A POOF

'Gross,' said someone. Simon Oliphant, I think it was.

'Gross to be a poof,' said Bonehead.

I wouldn't have put it past Bonehead to be the one that did it. I discussed it later, with Mark. Mark said he'd been doing some thinking over the weekend, about Hannah and Lars and stuff like that, and he reckoned that while he wouldn't personally want to be gay, and was sincerely glad that he wasn't gay, and certainly wouldn't come out and tell anyone if he *was* gay, since he didn't see any point in setting yourself up as a target, nonetheless he thought that people should live and let live, because what difference did it make to the rest of us if Lars Kennedy was the other way?

I agreed that it didn't really make any difference at all, except (though I didn't say this to Mark) it meant I could stop worrying about my mum.

Mark said his only irritation was that he'd had to brag about it.

'Like it's something to be proud of.'

Remembering what Mum had said, I told Mark that Lars probably hadn't seen it as bragging; more as making a statement.

'Standing up and being counted kind of thing.'

If I'd said that to Bonehead or the Mutant they'd most likely have torn into me. They'd have started jeering and making insinuations.

'Sticking up for the brown hatter!'

'Sure you aren't one yourself, Jo-ly?'

But then I probably wouldn't ever have said it to Bonehead or the Mutant, for that very reason. I'm quite pusillanimous, which is another word for cowardly which I have recently learnt. It is a good word, pusillanimous. Yellow and yucky, like stuff that comes out of spots. I was very yellow and yucky at that stage in my life.

Fortunately Mark isn't like Bonehead and the rest. I took a chance, 'cos I felt that he mightn't be.

He didn't jeer. He took it quite seriously and said, 'Yes…I can sort of see where he's at. Like if that's the way he is, that's the way he is, and why should he have to live a lie?'

I thought that was pretty good and later on told it to Rosa, who agreed with me.

'Someone who *thinks*,' she said, like it was something unusual. Which I guess it was. Specially at Hadley.

Monday was the day that Bonehead's dad was coming in to have his word with Fanny and try to get either Hannah or Mr Pelham, or maybe both of them, into trouble. Way back on Friday I think probably I'd have wanted him to succeed; but I'd had time to think about things. I'd talked to Rosa, I'd talked to Mark, I'd heard Mum, and now I wasn't so sure. Old Hannah hadn't been such a bad sort; I mean, she was entitled to her opinions. You had to admire her, the way she stuck to her guns. It didn't necessarily mean you had to *agree* with her. And Mr Pelham was way one of the best teachers we'd ever had. I wouldn't want him being given the elbow!

Next morning, which was Tuesday, a special assembly was called for everyone except Year Seven. I guess they were considered too young and were going to be talked at separately. Mr Hussey, our form teacher, told us that 'The Head will address you all at 11 o'clock.'

We knew what he was going to address us about, or at any rate we had a pretty good idea. The graffiti had been removed from the bog wall, but more had appeared in the showers. You don't expect graffiti at a school like Hadley. After all, our parents pay for us to go there: we're supposed to be *nice*. Not like the common sort of boy that goes to the comprehensive. (I put this bit in for Rosa. It is irony.* I think.)

We could see at once, from the way he twitched his robes, I mean his gown, that Fanny was in a lather. It had come to his attention, he said (only he said it a bit more long-winded and pompous than I'm saying it) that a guest speaker had engaged with us in discussion about – he hissed this next bit – *deviant sexuality*, and had tried to persuade us that this was cool, this was OK, this was acceptable. Well, it was not! It was an

* Could just be sarcasm?

aberration that must be abhorrent to every decent-minded person. It went against the norm, it went against the teachings of the church, and it was to be in every possible way deplored and discouraged. Not only deplored and discouraged but *actively condemned.*

He thundered this last bit out like a buffalo in a sexual frenzy. (As I imagine a buffalo in a sexual frenzy, never having actually seen one.) His face went all red and mottled, and his eyes all piggy, and his jowls slapped to and fro. Boy, was it impressive!

Anyone that was unfortunate enough, roared Fanny, to feel stirrings of such unnatural tendencies, should take himself in hand *right there and then.*

That is what he said. That is what he actually said. Take himself in hand. And nobody laughed. Nobody even sniggered. You'd better believe it. When Fanny went on the rampage, everyone dived for cover. But I was watching some of the staff, sitting in a semi-circle on the platform, and I just had this feeling that one or two of them weren't too happy with what was being said. I couldn't see Noah or Lars Kennedy, they were somewhere up at the back, but I couldn't help wondering how Lars was feeling, what with everyone knowing about him, and Fanny bawling on about the wrath of God. (The wrath of God definitely came into it somewhere, it's just I can't quite remember where.)

He yammered on for several minutes more, all about the fabric of society and the sanctity of family life, and how all this deviant sexual behaviour was threatening to pull it apart. He didn't tell us how it was threatening to pull it apart; just that it was. Like the world was full of dangerous deviants out to do us down, and we all had to be vigilant and keep a watch out for them before they could destroy our way of life.

It made me a bit uncomfortable, to tell you the truth. I kept thinking about Lars, and how he must be feeling. Sitting there like a dangerous deviant when he'd probably always reckoned he was much the same as anyone else except he just didn't happen to fancy girls. And now suddenly he was like some kind of hate figure at the top of everyone's hit list. Pretty scary!

Fanny went rambling on. Another thing that had come to his attention, he said, was that some person, or persons, had been defacing school property with vile and objectionable graffiti. This had got to stop! We did not do this sort of thing at Hadley. If people wished to voice their opinions, or to vent their feelings, they must find another way of doing so.

'I will not tolerate vandalism! I trust I make myself clear?'

Phew! And how. We left the hall feeling quite subdued, though it didn't take long for Bonehead to get his act together.

'That was my dad,' he boasted. 'Coming in and talking to him. It was my dad brought all that on! I reckon someone's going to get the boot.'

By someone, he meant Mr Pelham. I felt that if Mr Pelham were to be sacked it would definitely be unfair, though I couldn't quite work out why. After all, he *had* been the one to invite Hannah into school, and Hannah *had* tried to persuade us that being gay was acceptable, which it obviously wasn't. I didn't care what Rosa said. I mean, I didn't believe all that hellfire and damnation stuff that had come spewing out of Fanny. I didn't believe that people like Lars were a threat to society, but I did sort of believe that what they did should be condemned. Well, maybe not condemned, exactly, but definitely discouraged. I mean, they shouldn't be all upfront and in your face about it. I wasn't saying they had to live a *lie*, but why couldn't Lars have just kept quiet? Why did he feel the need to go making statements? That was what bugged me!

Mum and Dad were both out when I got home. My first thought was to go round and see Rosa and tell her what had happened, but then Noah came in and I tried to talk to him about it, only he wouldn't.

'We've already had a bellyful,' he said. 'Do we have to go through it all over again?'

'I just wondered how you felt,' I said.

'Bored,' said Noah, 'if you must know. Why don't you trot round to your girlfriend and have a nice cosy chat with her about it?'

''Cos I just remembered, she's staying late at school.' And then, greatly daring, I said, 'How's *your* girlfriend?'

But he didn't want to talk about that, either. We'd had just the one moment of being close, the first of its kind in all our lives; and it didn't look like we'd be having any more. I reckoned he'd probably regretted it the minute he opened his mouth. He probably looked on it as a weakness. Guys don't talk about that kind of thing; not that way, they don't. They talk about who they've scored with and who's an easy lay. Least, if

Bonehead and the Mutant are anything to go by. Not that Bonehead and the Mutant are my role models, you understand. But even me and Mark, who are pretty good mates, even we wouldn't talk about being in love, so I knew with Noah it wasn't something he was likely to repeat.

I didn't push him as I thought maybe things had gone wrong somewhere, like maybe he and his girl had had a quarrel and broken up, or something. He'd seemed a bit down, just lately. Like one time when me and Rosa seriously fell out and didn't speak to each other for almost a week. I was nearly suicidal!

So I just said, like, 'OK, forget I asked,' in what I hoped were conciliatory tones, except they obviously weren't 'cos Noah snaps, 'Why can't people just mind their own damn business?'

'Hey,' I cry, 'chill out, man!' to which Noah goes, 'Don't you patronise me, you little turd!' and bangs out of the room. *Again.* This is the second time he's banged out of the room. This is definitely not a normal pattern of behaviour. Girlfriend trouble, for sure! I recognise the signs.

Over tea I told Mum and Dad about Fanny's rant. How he'd thundered on about hellfire and damnation and deviant sexual behaviour. How it not only had to be deplored and discouraged but, *'Actively condemned,'* I bawled, in an apoplectic Fanny-type of bellow.

I told them about the graffiti, and how 'We do not do that sort of thing at Hadley,' and if people wished to vent their feelings they had better find some other way of doing it.

Mum and Dad listened in a kind of appalled silence. It wasn't until I got to the bit about people venting their feelings that they came to life.

'He said *that?'* said Mum. 'He actually *said that?'*

'I can't believe it,' said Dad.

'He did,' I said. 'Honest! Didn't he?'

I turned to Noah, who nodded.

'He actually said—' it seemed that Mum couldn't believe it, either – 'he actually said *"vent their feelings"*? In *"Some other way"*?'

'Instead of defacing school property.'

'This is outrageous! A *headteacher?* In this day and age? What a redneck!'

'He did get pretty red,' I said. 'I thought he was going to have a coronary, or something.'

'Was Lars there?' said Mum.

'I dunno,' I said. 'I s'pose so.'

'Was he?' Mum also turned to Noah. He

nodded again. 'For God's sake! That poor lad! I must ring him!' She pushed back her chair and shot to her feet. 'No! I can't!' She plummeted back down again. 'His mother might pick up the phone. She'd wonder who I am...some strange woman wanting to speak to her son. I don't think he's told her...Noah! You do it.'

'Me?' Noah sounded alarmed.

'Yes! Why not? You're supposed to be his friend.'

'They're not *friends*,' I said; but Mum just rode right over the top of me. I don't think she even heard. I don't think she was even listening.

'Ask him round for that meal! This time I mean it. Don't you think?' She swung back to Dad. 'Ask him round?'

'Let me just get this straight,' said Dad. 'You're telling me that Mr Fanshawe knew about the graffiti, which meant he must have known about Lars. Right? So he gets up in front of the whole school—'

'Not Year Seven,' I said; but it seemed Dad wasn't listening to me, either.

'–in front of the *whole school* and practically incites them to violence? This is utterly unbelievable!'

'It's more than unbelievable,' said Mum. 'It's

totally unacceptable! I'm not having my sons subjected to this kind of bigoted blimpery!'

'You're not going to go in and talk to him?' I said. I found this distinctly unnerving. If word got out, my life would be unbearable! Bonehead would never let me live it down.

'I'm certainly not just going to sit back and do nothing,' said Mum.

'But it isn't anything to *do* with you!' I said.

'No, it's not!' Noah suddenly came to life, jumping in to my rescue. 'Just let things alone! It's over – it's finished! Forget about it!'

'*Forget?* You're asking me to *forget?*'

'He's asking you not to rock any boats,' said Dad.

'Well, I'm sorry, but there are times when boats have to be rocked! He can't be allowed to get away with this sort of thing! Unless—'

Mum stopped. Her eyes met Dad's across the table.

'Unless—'

'What?' I said. 'What?'

'Unless we...' Mum raised an eyebrow. Dad nodded.

'Why not?'

Sometimes it's like they can read each other's

mind. I guess it comes from living together for so long.

'Who should it be?' said Mum.

'Not one of us.'

'No. I agree.'

'How about Mick?'

Mick Davies was one of Dad's fellow presenters. Not the nerdy one. Mick Davies did the morning slot, from nine till midday. What Dad had wanted was the one after. Twelve till two. He and Mick were good buddies.

'You're going to put it on the radio?' I said, excitedly.

The radio was different! Especially if Mick Davies was the one to do it. Not even Bonehead could blame me for something that Mick Davies chose to do.

'You're going to do a phone-in?'

'We're going to do something,' said Mum.

'Your mum's right,' said Dad. 'We can't just sit back and ignore it simply because we have two sons at the school.'

'*Especially* as we have two sons at the school.'

'This is brilliant!' I said. I really went for the idea. All I could think was, 'Fanny's going to get worked over!' and then Noah burst back into the conversation.

'What is it with you media people? Can't you ever respect anyone's privacy? What's it got to *do* with you? Why can't you just let it drop, when I ask you?' And then he turns on me and goes, 'And you! What the hell did you have to tell them for in the first place? You know what they're like!'

'What are we like?' says Mum, a bit frosty.

'You're like paparazzi! You're like doorsteppers!'

Dad bridled. 'I resent that! This is a matter of principle. We're not intruding on anyone's privacy.'

'Yes, you are! You're intruding on mine. I have to go to this blasted school!'

'I thought you used to like it,' said Mum, in hurt tones.

'There's nothing wrong with the school,' said Dad, 'just the lunatic who's running it. He wasn't there when we chose the place, so don't go getting on our case!'

'Someone's got to take up the cudgels,' said Mum. 'Don't you realise what he's doing? He's making that poor boy's life a misery!'

'Yes,' said Noah, 'and you'll make our lives a misery!'

'Noah, I'm sorry, but this sort of thing, this—'

Mum waved a hand, '—*Nazi propaganda* is dangerous. It needs to be exposed. The man is not fit to be in charge of young minds. He's like some kind of fascist thug!'

'That's right, he is, and it's bad enough we have to live with him,' snarled Noah, 'without you and Dad going and making an issue of it!'

That was the third time Noah went slamming out of the room. It was getting to be a habit.

Mum stared after him, bewildered. 'What is his problem?' she said.

'I think he's had a quarrel with his girlfriend,' I said.

'*Another* girlfriend?' said Mum.

'This one was serious…he was in love with her.'

'Really?' For a moment it looked as though Mum might be going to let herself be sidetracked. Noah in love! 'I didn't know about this! Who was she?'

'Dunno. He wouldn't say. He didn't want people taking the piss.'

'And you think they've quarrelled?'

'I reckon so.'

'Well, I'm sorry if he's upset,' said Mum, 'but it was bound to happen sooner or later.'

She said that Noah had broken enough hearts

in his time; he couldn't hope to get away with it indefinitely.

'No one remains immune for ever. I'm sure he's suffering, but that's no reason for grossly anti-social behaviour. And it's *certainly* no reason for letting some bigoted old blimp get away with raging homophobia. For goodness' sake!' said Mum. 'This is going back to the days of the lynch mob!'

chapter nine

There was a strange atmosphere round school in the days following Fanny's outburst; strange, and a bit scary. Nothing that you could immediately put your finger on. Like a thick black river of pus, oozing and sliming somewhere beneath the floorboards. Something you could sense, but not actually see.

And then, now and again, you heard things. Things that were said. Things that were hinted. Lars was still there, walking round like nothing had ever happened, but there was this space around him. You never saw him with anyone else; not even Noah, who had been his friend. Though not his special friend. I kept reminding myself of this. It wasn't like Noah was being disloyal, or anything. They'd never been close.

One day when a bunch of us were barrelling

along the corridor we passed Lars coming the other way. He nodded at me, same as usual, and I didn't know what to do or where to look. I knew that I ought to acknowledge him, I mean, I knew that's what Rosa would say, so I just, kind of, twisted my mouth and made a mumbling sound.

In a loud voice, as we moved on down the corridor, the Mutant said, 'You wanna watch it, Jo-ly! Talking to a brown hatter like that.'

I know that what I'm going to say is unworthy, but I did wish Lars could have just ignored me. 'Cos after that, Bonehead and the Mutant got this thing going where they pretended that Lars Kennedy fancied me. They started calling me the Brown Hatter's toy boy, and stuff like that. So from that point on, if ever I caught a glimpse of him, I got out of the way, pronto. At least, I tried to.

The trouble with a school like Hadley – *one* of the troubles with a school like Hadley – it's so small you can't really help bumping into people. What I'm saying is, there isn't any easy way of avoiding them. Like at Combe Cross you could probably go weeks, if not the whole term, without meeting even half the people there. You probably wouldn't even know half the people. At Hadley, everyone knows everybody. And I bumped into Lars all the time.

There was this ditty going round the school:

The boy stood on the burning deck
His backside to the mast.
And he resolved to keep it there
Till Kennedy had passed.

Dorks like Bonehead and the Mutant took to chanting it under their breath whenever they saw Lars approaching. I never knew which way to look. I tried telling myself it was just a bit of harmless banter, no worse than the time they'd taken the piss out of me for kissing Rosa on Fidler's Hill; but I think inside myself I knew this wasn't true. They weren't just taking the piss, they were putting the boot in.

As time went on, they started to grow bolder. Lars was walking up the drive one morning as we were making our way over to the playing fields. The cry went up:

'Bums to the wall, lads! Brown Hatter's coming!'

Everyone except me and Mark rushed screaming into the flower beds and pressed themselves against the chapel wall. I could feel my face burning, bright red. This time, Lars didn't look at me. I guess he'd sussed that I'd rather he didn't. Or maybe what it was, they'd finally knocked the spirit out of him. I don't know. I just know that I felt terrible and didn't do a thing about it.

Nobody did a thing about it. Not then, not ever. Not any of the teachers. Mr Pelham might have done, if he'd been there, but he wasn't. (Rumour had it he'd been sacked, but he turned up again the following term so maybe it was just, like, a temporary suspension.) None of the rest of the staff seemed to notice; or if they did they turned a blind eye. I guess it was easier that way.

More graffiti appeared in the bog. This time it was done way down, and minuscule, on the cubicle walls, so you had to look really close to read it and the cleaner never noticed, which meant it stayed there. Stayed there, and got added to. You'd have thought someone might have taken a felt-tip pen, at least, and blocked it out, but nobody did. And that, of course, includes me.

Why didn't I? If it bothered me so much – and it did bother me – why didn't *I* block it out?

Why didn't Noah? Why didn't anyone?

Why didn't Lars?

I've often wondered about this. I've often tried

to imagine how he must have felt, reading those things about himself. 'Cos I'm sure he must have seen them. Why didn't *he* block them out?

All I can think is, it must have been a sort of pride. Pride mixed with defiance. The same thing as made him come out in the first place. You'd have to feel pretty sure of yourself, I'd say, to do a thing like that.

I wouldn't! But I am not at all brave.

Meanwhile, the black pus went on oozing, and if I could sense it then Lars must have sensed it, too. However sure of himself he may have been, he could hardly fail to notice all the hints and innuendo. You'd have to be blind as a bat not to see Bonehead and the Mutant pressing their bums to the wall, and deaf as a post not to hear their chanting. And they weren't the only ones; just the most obvious. Even little kids in Year Seven, kids that had only been at the school five minutes, could be seen giggling. The Upper School didn't giggle, and they didn't chant or press their bums to the wall. But they didn't exactly rally round in support. Whenever you saw Lars, he was on his own. They even, subtly, managed to put a space between him and themselves when they were in assembly. Noah was always way down, at the end of the row. But he and Lars had never been buddies. Not close.

Sometimes even then I used to wonder how Lars must be feeling. How he had the guts to just carry on the way he was. I kept thinking that I wouldn't have done, if I'd been in his position, though when I stopped to think about what I might have done instead I realised that perhaps he didn't have much choice. He couldn't just bunk off school; not indefinitely. Not unless he confided in his mum and dad, which I afterwards learnt that he didn't. Lars's mum and dad were completely in the dark. They sort of half knew about him being gay, but they knew nothing about him coming out. They had no idea how he was being treated. Jeered at, and ostracised. He kept it all to himself. Just suffered in silence.

Dad's mate, Mick Davies, had done his phone-in about Fanny's outburst, but Lars's mum and dad hadn't heard it. It was a bit of a wash-out, in any case. I missed it, on account of being at school, but Mum and Dad listened in. It got them pretty mad. They said whenever you did phone-ins on any subject that was connected with s.e.x., 'all the rednecks and the bigots come crawling out of the woodwork.' There'd been lots of people who had actually *supported* Fanny. Dad fumed and railed on about mental dwarves, and Mum said how it would be different if we lived in London, but I thought that in London it probably wouldn't have happened in the first place. I couldn't imagine a school in London ever having a headmaster like Fanny.

I said this to Mark, and he said, 'Why not?' and I thought about it and said, 'Well, because London's probably full of guys that are gay. I mean, like, it's probably quite normal down there. Come out down there, it'd be no big deal. Up here it's like – wow! Cross-dressing, or something.'

'Worse,' said Mark.

'Worse,' I said. 'I wouldn't do it, would you?'

Mark said no way.

'I reckon you'd have to be pretty thick-skinned. Up here.'

Mark agreed. He said he didn't hold it against Lars that he was gay, because live and let live and it takes all sorts, but he didn't think it was necessary to go round making statements about it. 'He obviously doesn't give a toss what people think.'

'He couldn't,' I said, 'or he wouldn't have done it.'

This way, it made it seem not quite so bad, what

was happening. Lars had brought it all on himself, and he didn't give a toss. Which was just as well, since days passed and turned into weeks and still nobody was lifting a finger to do anything about it. I kept thinking that surely they would, but they never did. It was like all the staff were wearing blinkers and ear plugs. I guess they simply preferred not to notice. I mean, it wasn't like anyone was actually being physically violent. The lynch mob was strictly verbal.

Everyone knows the rhyme about sticks and stones:

> *Sticks and stones may break my bones*
> *But names will never hurt me.*

So that was OK. At least, that was what I told myself. I didn't discuss it with Rosa; she was too censorious. Me and Mark, we understood about these things. We didn't *condemn;* but we certainly didn't condone. I felt comfortable, talking with Mark.

From time to time, Mum would ask me, 'How are things? Is everything all right?' I knew that what she was really asking was, How are things with Lars? Is Lars all right? And I always said they were OK, because, I mean, no one was beating up on him or anything like that. You heard of gangs going out gay-bashing, but that wasn't happening to Lars. Just a bit of name-calling was all.

Mum sighed and said she supposed that was inevitable.

'But nothing too bad?' she insisted.

And I just mumbled. 'Cos the one thing I most desperately didn't want was Mum coming into school and making waves.

She never asked Noah how things were going. Noah didn't really communicate with us any more. A grunt was the most you ever got out of him – when he was there to grunt, that is. We only ever seemed to see him at breakfast. He spent the early part of every evening at the Sports Centre, and the later part up in his room. When Mum said why didn't he come down and be sociable, he snapped that he'd got homework to do.

'Girlfriend trouble,' I said.

'It's really hit him hard, hasn't it?' said Mum. 'I'm almost tempted to say it serves him right…getting a taste of his own medicine at last! Never mind. He'll get over it!'

chapter ten

It was one afternoon, in the village, when I met Lars again on my own.

I'd got off the bus and wandered over to the newsagent's to buy a packet of crisps. There were a gang of kids in there, four of them. Year Sevens, they looked like. Two of them were local; I didn't recognise the other two. They were giving the guy who ran the place a rough time. Mr Ansari, his name was. He's not there any more; he only lasted about six months. The fact is, I have to be honest, our village isn't used to what they call 'coloured folk'. They're pretty racist in these parts. I guess it comes from being isolated.

The kids had obviously been making a nuisance of themselves and Mr Ansari had told them to get out, or to leave things alone, and they'd taken exception. As I walked in, the abuse was flying. I heard one kid shout, 'Paki scum!'

I knew I ought to say something, but as I believe I've already mentioned I am rather pusillanimous. I am not proud of this; it is just a fact of life. Plus there were four of them, and they were all pretty big. I mean, I would have said something if they'd threatened physical violence. I wouldn't just have stood by; I'm not as pusillanimous as all that. What I'd have done, I'd probably have gone for help.

So I'm standing there thinking about it, dithering what to do, when all of a sudden Lars is in the shop. He's telling the kids to piss off, and surprise surprise, they're actually doing it! They're giving him a load of mouth, but they're doing it. As they move in a sullen heap towards the door, one of them turns and sticks up two fingers.

'Paki bastard!'

All I can say is, it wasn't one of the kids from the village. Not that that makes it any better. Lars was on him in a flash. He picked him up by the scruff of his neck and literally booted him out on to the pavement. Noah would have done the same if he'd been there. I know he would. But Noah wasn't there. Lars was, and it was Lars that did it.

It was kind of awkward after that. Knowing how to behave. Like whether to talk about it or try to pretend it had never happened.

Mr Ansari said, 'Hooligans!' You could see he was shaken. Lars suggested he should call the police, but he didn't seem too keen on that idea. He never wanted trouble, Mr Ansari. He just wanted to get on and do his job and be left alone. Some hopes!

Next thing, I found myself outside, with Lars. I didn't have to have waited for him. I mean, I was the one that had gone in there first, so naturally I was the one that was served first. I could just have scarpered without saying anything; but it didn't seem right. Not after what he'd done. So I hung around, waiting for him, and as he came out I said, 'Gross!'

Lars didn't say anything; just very slightly inclined his head.

'I don't think Mr Ansari comes from Pakistan anyway,' I said.

Lars said, 'No?'

'I don't think so,' I said.

'Well, there you go,' said Lars.

We went on for a bit in silence. Not exactly what you would call a companionable sort of silence, but I suppose it hardly could have been. I mean, there wasn't any reason Lars would want to converse with me. Not any more. Not after all that had happened, at school and everything. But you can't just walk in a vacuum!

'I suppose you don't get that kind of thing where you come from?' I babbled.

Lars stopped, and looked at me. He said, 'Prejudice is everywhere – and it is always gross.'

And then he turned, abruptly, and peeled off down Carter's Lane towards the Common.

I remember thinking about that other time we'd bumped into each other; the time with the badger. How Lars had told me about loving animals and losing his cat and how devastated he'd been. And I remember this huge feeling of – sadness, I suppose it was, washing over me, because I knew he'd never ever talk to me like that again. It was like something had gone from my life that I hadn't even realised was there.

When I got home I found that Noah had arrived ahead of me. I don't know where Mum was. Up in the attics, or something.

'I've just been to the newsagent's,' I said. 'Some kids were bad-mouthing Mr Ansari. Making racist remarks. You know?'

'I hope you gave them what for?' said Noah.

'Lars did,' I said. 'He told them to piss off. He actually picked one kid up and threw him out the shop!'

I waited for Noah to be impressed; but all he said, rather stiffly, was, 'Bully for Lars.'

'Why is everyone being so horrible to him?' It just, like, burst out of me. I hadn't planned on saying it.

'I wasn't aware that everyone was being horrible,' said Noah.

'They are!' I cried. 'You know they are! And no one's doing anything to stop it!'

'So what do you expect me to do?' said Noah.

I guess what I expected him to do was what he'd done for me, when I was little and weedy: I expected him to stand up for Lars. I didn't expect him to behave the same as all the others!

I started to try and say something, but Mum walked in and the moment was gone. I did make a sort of attempt, a bit later. We passed on the stairs, me going up, Noah going down, on his way out to the Sports Club. I got as far as saying, 'Noah—'

'Joel, just shut up,' said Noah. 'Do you hear me? Just SHUT UP!'

OK. So I got the message, loud and clear: he didn't want to talk about it. Fine by me. I didn't want to talk about it, either. It made me uncomfortable, to tell the truth. I didn't know why I'd brought it up in the first place.

Noah apologised to me next day. He said, 'I'm sorry I bawled you out.'

''S all right,' I said.

'No, it's not,' said Noah.

'Well!' I shrugged. It wouldn't be the first time.

'The thing is—' Noah stopped. 'It's just – I – I can't – what I mean – oh, shit!' He scrunched his fingers through his hair. 'I don't know what I'm trying to say!'

I told him again that it was all right. I really didn't want him to go on. I didn't want confessions! Like yes-you-were-right-I-have-been-horrible-to-Lars. That kind of thing.

'Just forget it,' I said.

'Well—' He hesitated. I got the feeling he really did want to say something; he just couldn't find the words. 'OK. But I'm sorry I yelled at you!'

So that was our attempt at talking. After which I let it alone, and so did Noah; and things went on just the same as before.

The river of pus went on oozing, thicker,

blacker, more menacing than ever. So thick by now it was almost like engine oil. Dark, evil-smelling; turgid and festering.

I'm sure, if an outsider had come into school, they would have sensed it immediately. You could almost reach out and touch it. The smell of it clogged your nostrils. But Fanny still reigned supreme; and the staff still covered their eyes and blocked their ears; and the rest of us did the same.

And Lars battled on, totally alone, until in the end it became too much for him.

It was on the Thursday I'd bumped into him in the newsagent's; the following afternoon when Noah and I made our feeble efforts at conversation.

That was the day, that Friday, when Lars took his dog for a walk across the Common and his dog came back without him.

chapter eleven

The first we knew was when Mr Kennedy rang to ask if Lars was at our place. He thought perhaps he might have called round to see Noah.

It was me that answered the phone (I'd thought it was going to be Rosa). I didn't tell him that Lars and Noah weren't really buddies and that there wasn't any reason for Lars to be at our place. In any case, it wouldn't have accounted for Dolph turning up by himself. Lars was devoted to his dog! He'd never have let him go running off.

'I'll get Mum,' I said. I went bawling off up the hall.

'*Mu-u-u-m!* It's Mr Kennedy!'

'Mr Who?' said Mum.

'Mr Kennedy! Lars's dad. Lars went out and hasn't come back and it's over three hours ago and he's worried that something might have happened.'

Mum said, 'Oh, God!' and shot off up the hall.

Seconds later, she was back.

'I'm going to get the car out! Go upstairs and tell Noah I want him to come with me.'

'Why?' I said. 'Where are you going?'

'Going to help look for Lars.'

'You don't think something's happened to him?'

'I don't know. I hope to God not!'

Mum pushed past me. 'Can I come?' I yelled.

'No, you stay here. Go and tell Noah!'

I galloped up the stairs and burst into Noah's room. Noah was lying on his bed, with his headphones on.

'What do you want?' he said. We don't normally go crashing into each other's rooms.

I gabbled at him about Lars.

'You don't think anything's happened to him, do you?'

'Like what?' said Noah.

'Like...I dunno! Like he's been lynched, or something?'

Noah shoved me to one side.

'Don't be so bloody stupid!'

'He could have been!' I bawled it at him as he disappeared down the stairs. 'The way people have been behaving!'

Mum and Noah went off, leaving me in the house by myself. Dad, of course, was doing his radio programme. After a bit of dithering, I picked up the phone and rang Rosa. I don't quite know what made me do it. Force of habit, I guess. But it wasn't just to gossip! I think what it was, I was suddenly scared. I needed her to reassure me. Nothing could have happened to Lars!

Rosa came round immediately.

'How long did you say he'd been gone?'

'Three hours,' I said.

'*Three hours?* Just walking?'

'Over three hours. And Dolph came back without him!'

'That is worrying,' said Rosa.

If Lars had been planning something – like running away, or something – he'd have taken Dolph with him. Either that or left him at home. He would never just have abandoned him.

I told Rosa about the incident with Mr Ansari, and Lars saying afterwards that prejudice was everywhere – and that it was always gross.

'I used to think he wasn't bothered. You know?

Like…that was the way he came across. Mr Cool. Couldn't care less. But when he said that, about prejudice—'

It hadn't struck me at the time; I'd been too busy, worrying what to talk about. Now it all came back to me. His face, drawn and taut; his voice, carefully expressionless, with that slight sing-song Swedish accent.

'It was really getting to him!'

'Let's play Scrabble,' said Rosa. 'Take our mind off things.'

We tried, but we really couldn't concentrate. Even Rosa found it difficult. We kept fidgeting, and glancing at the clock, and listening for the sound of car tyres on the gravel.

It was dark when Mum and Noah arrived home. You only had to look at their faces to know that the news was not good.

'Mum?' I said.

'D-did you f-find him?' stammered Rosa. It's not very often that Rosa stammers. She's usually very together.

'Yes,' said Mum. 'We found him.'

'Is he…' I couldn't bring myself to ask the question. Rosa had to do it for me.

'Is he all right?'

Slowly, Mum shook her head. She put a hand to her mouth.

'Give me a minute. Just give me a minute! Joel, get me a drink, there's a sweetie.'

I rushed to the drinks cabinet. Noah made to leave the room.

'Noah, don't go!' Mum almost wailed it. 'Stay with us! Don't go off by yourself! Not now! Have something to drink. Have a brandy! Joel—'

'I'm OK.' Noah turned, and went through the door. He didn't slam it this time. We heard him going up the stairs.

'Oh, God!'

Mum half-started from her seat, then fell back again. Rosa was chewing at a thumbnail. I sloshed whisky into a glass and rushed back across the room with it. I don't know how people drink that stuff. I'm sure they don't like it; they always pull these agonised faces as it goes down.

Mum took a big gulp. Her face was agonised to begin with.

'Mum?' I said. 'Mum?'

'Oh, Joel!' She gave this little laugh; but not like she thought anything was funny. 'I'm supposed to be in the business of helping people, aren't I? I'm supposed to give them good advice! Instead of which—' She took a breath, deep and quivering. 'I should have known! I should have known! I rang him after – that day. When we talked. I took a chance. I – got his mum. I – said I – wanted to speak to him about...media studies.' Mum's hand was shaking. She pushed her hair back.

'He came to the phone. He assured me he was all right! He said he was coping. He said...he didn't feel he had anything to be ashamed of. I told him that he hadn't. But I told him – if he wanted to – come and talk...he said he didn't need it. He said he was just going to stick it out. He sounded so...so positive! But I should have known!' cried Mum. 'He was only Noah's age. I should have known!'

I thought of Lars as I had last seen him, only that morning, golden and glowing, striding down the corridor with that space around him, like he was a giant amongst pygmies.

There was silence.

'Mrs Bradbeer?' Rosa said it timidly. 'What – what exactly—'

'Oh, Rosa!' Mum's voice was just a whisper. 'Don't ask me! Please don't ask me!' And then she suddenly sat up, very straight. 'No, I'm sorry! I shouldn't have said that. That's wrong of me.

Of course you have to know! Let me just – get my act together. Just—'

'It's all right,' I said. 'If you'd rather not tell us.'

Mum shook her head.

'You'll find out sooner or later. It's better you hear it from me. I just hope—' She gave us this watery smile. 'I just hope you're feeling strong!'

We both said we were, though my stomach was churning.

'Well, then.' Mum took another gulp of whisky. 'We found him in – one of the – little spinneys. He—'

I don't know how to write this next bit. I don't want to write it.

Mum didn't want to tell it.

Me and Rosa didn't want to hear it. But as Mum said, we would have found out sooner or later.

'He – used his tie,' she said. 'And the dog's lead.' Rosa's hand reached out for mine and held it, very tightly. 'It was – Noah who – who f—' Mum broke off. 'Noah! I must go to him!' She jumped up, splashing whisky over the floor. 'He shouldn't be on his own!'

Mum went flying from the room. I was shaking all over. Lars is dead. Lars is dead. Lars is dead. The words went thudding like drumbeats through my brain.

'Joel!' Rosa slid down beside me on the sofa. 'Don't! Don't torture yourself!'

I couldn't speak. I couldn't stop shaking. I kept seeing Lars, striding down that corridor. For the first time ever, he hadn't acknowledged me. Always before, he'd nodded or said hi or raised a hand. But not this morning.

'Listen,' said Rosa, 'it wasn't your fault! There was nothing you could have done. It was Fanny! Poisoning people's minds!'

I knew she was only trying to comfort me. I knew she wanted me to talk, but I just couldn't. All I could see was Lars, striding down the corridor; and all I could think was, what harm had he ever done? And how he had loved his dog. How only a sense of utter desolation could have pushed him into leaving it behind.

Rosa stayed with me until Mum came back down. Mum was worried. She said she couldn't get Noah to talk.

'But he must do! He can't keep it all bottled up.'

She wondered if perhaps he might talk to me.

'After all, you're his brother.'

I could have told her that Noah wouldn't. We'd made that one feeble attempt – just this morning, which already seemed like weeks ago. All we'd managed to do was embarrass ourselves.

'Try,' urged Mum. 'Give it a go!'

I knocked on his door as I went upstairs, and he said to come in, but then I got tongue-tied. Noah said, 'I suppose Mum sent you.'

'She's worried,' I said.

'About me?'

I nodded.

'What's she worried about me for?'

I humped a shoulder. 'I dunno.'

'I'm OK,' said Noah. 'How about you? Are you OK?'

I tried to say that I was, but then it just kind of burst out of me. 'It's so awful! I can't believe it! It's just so awful!'

As soon as I said it, he clammed up.

'I don't want to talk about it.'

'But—'

'If you want to talk, you can do it with Mum. She likes that sort of thing. Go and chew it over with her.'

'B—'

'Joel! I mean it. Just go away and leave me alone!'

I said again, 'But M—'

'JOEL!' For a moment I thought he was going to hit me. Then instead he sank down on to his bed and I knew that he wasn't going to hit me, he was going to cry. If I didn't get out, he was actually going to cry.

I'd never seen my brother cry. It wasn't something I wanted to witness.

'Please,' he whispered. 'Please! Just leave me alone!'

What could I do? You can't make people talk. Not if they don't want to.

I went back downstairs to tell Mum.

'He doesn't want to talk about it. But he says he's OK.'

'Of course he's not OK!' snapped Mum. 'How can he be OK?' And then I think maybe I must have looked a bit hurt, or a bit stricken, or something, because she flung both arms round me and said, 'Oh, Joel, I'm sorry! Forgive me! I'm sure you did your best. Why is it,' she cried, 'that the men of this family find it so difficult to show their feelings?'

chapter twelve

Next day, at school, Fanny called us in for another special assembly. All except Year Sevens. The news hadn't yet broken, so Noah and I were the only ones who knew what it was about. I tried to catch Noah's eye as I came into the hall, but he wouldn't look at me. He must have known that I was there. The sixth form all sat at the back, on chairs, while the rest of us filed past on our way to the front. I wondered if I was the only one to notice the empty seat where Lars should have been.

Mark hissed, 'I bet it's about the graffiti.' He'd told me that on his way home last night he'd found some new stuff under the arch at Hoxley Bridge. Whoever was doing it was starting to get bold. They'd spray-canned it in letters half a metre high. I won't say what they'd written as I think it would be classed as obscene, and in any case it would be a desecration. To Lars's memory, I mean. I couldn't help wondering if he'd seen it. He would have had to go under Hoxley Bridge to reach the Common. Was that, in the end, what had broken him? He'd seemed so strong! Didn't give a toss. But all the time, inside himself, he'd obviously been hurting. And some of us had gone on jeering, and the rest of us had gone on looking the other way; and while our backs were turned, Lars had taken that final step.

I didn't tell Mark what had happened, even though he was my friend. I left that to Fanny.

A sort of shock wave went round the hall when he broke the news. You could actually feel it, pressing on your eardrums. You could even hear it. The mass intake of breath, and then – silence. Complete and total.

Fanny gave us a minute or so to absorb what we'd just heard, and then started burbling. He did it in his usual pompous fashion, but burble was all it amounted to. He said how Lars had only recently joined the school, how perhaps he had found it difficult to settle, to make friends.

'And so we have the tragedy of a young man's life being prematurely ended. His stay with us was pitifully short! He was a student of great promise.

Exceptional ability. He had a brilliant future before him, and he will be sorely missed, for even in his brief time at Hadley he made his mark. And yet sadly, here in our midst, he obviously felt isolated. Maybe even rejected. He felt – albeit mistakenly – that there was no one to whom he could turn. No one to confide in. And this – *this* – is where the tragedy lies, for—'

We never knew how Fanny was going to end his sentence. I'm not even sure that everyone was properly taking it in; I think most people were too stunned. In any case, it was nothing but empty mouthings. What Mum would have called humbug. But at that moment there was an eruption from somewhere at the back of the hall, and next thing I knew Noah had jumped up on stage and was practically elbowing Fanny out of the way.

'Bullshit! This is all bullshit! Lars didn't just *feel* rejected, he *was* rejected. By everyone! Every single one of us!'

Fanny opened his mouth to bleat a protest, but Noah was in full flood. I don't think anything could have stopped him at that point. The odd thing was, nobody tried to. Not one member of staff came to Fanny's aid. Fanny himself made a feeble move in Noah's direction, but

Noah simply shook him off.

'Lars was my friend! And I let him down. We all let him down! But me, more than anyone. I betrayed him!'

Fanny made another abortive attempt at interrupting. Noah spun round, shooting a finger into his chest so that he went staggering backwards.

'Yes, and so did you! You betrayed everything you're supposed to stand for! But I betrayed a friend. Lars was brave enough to speak out. He stood up and said, this is me, this is the way I am. He wanted us both to do it, only I didn't have the guts. So for what it's worth, I'm doing it now! And you can treat me the way you treated him, you can jeer, you can sneer, you can call me names. You can chalk up all the obscenities you like, because I don't give a damn! Do you understand?' He said it directly to Fanny, spitting the words into his face. *I don't give a damn!*'

With that, he turned and left the stage. Left the stage, left the hall. After a moment's hesitation, Mr Phillips, the deputy head, got up and went after him. Fanny, plainly at a loss, stood before us like a deflated bladder. And this time the silence was electric.

I heard Mark, next to me, let out his breath in a

long 'Phew!' I can't remember what I was thinking; or even if I was thinking anything at all. It was like my brain had gone numb.

After what seemed like minutes, though I expect it was probably only seconds, Fanny dismissed us and we all trooped back to our classrooms. Nobody said very much, just at first. I think mostly we were too embarrassed, what with me being Noah's brother and all. I felt embarrassed. In my petty small-minded way, all I could think was, 'In front of everyone! Why did he have to do it in front of everyone?'

I was also still feeling terrible about what had happened to Lars. Everybody was. Not even Bonehead and the Mutant opened their great clanging mouths. They did later; but for the moment even they had been silenced.

At break time, I walked round the playing field with Mark. It never occurred to me to look for Noah. Maybe I should have done, just to show solidarity. But then again, maybe he wouldn't have wanted it.

'I reckon that was dead brave,' said Mark. 'Coming out like that.'

I felt this wave of gratitude wash over me.

'You reckon?'

'Standing up to Fanny the way he did...I reckon most people'll think he deserves a medal! Don't you think he deserves a medal?'

I didn't know what I thought. My brain was still in turmoil. I just could hardly bring myself to believe it. *Noah* – my *brother* – telling the whole school that he was gay!

'I guess it was a bit of a surprise?' said Mark. 'I mean—' He shot this look at me. 'I guess you didn't know about it?'

'No way!'

It was only now, looking back, that certain things fell into place. The look that had passed between Lars and Noah at Christmas, when Chloë had wanted to go off across the Common with them. They hadn't wanted her! They'd wanted to be on their own. And Noah taking Anna to the Victorian Evening. He could have taken Emily, but that would have seemed disloyal to Lars, maybe. So he'd taken Anna, because Anna wasn't any threat. And the conversation we'd had, the two of us, after New Year's. Our one and only intimate conversation.

'It's great, isn't it? Being in love!'

I could still hear him saying it. And I'd automatically assumed it was a girl he was talking about, because what else would I assume? He'd always gone with girls before.

'You don't reckon he'll get into a row?' I said. I mean, he'd actually shoved a finger into Fanny's chest. You don't do that sort of thing to headteachers. 'You don't reckon they'll give him the sack, or anything?'

'What, your brother? They'll more likely give Fanny the sack!'

I must have been looking a bit bothered, because Mark did something he'd never done before, he put an arm across my shoulders and said, 'It's cool, man! Just relax. The way he did it…that was really cool!'

By the start of afternoon school, Bonehead and the Mutant had managed to get their act together. Bonehead came up to me and in his hectoring way said, 'Tell me! Does it run in the family, Jo-ly?' The Mutant sniggered, and I felt like punching him. I felt like punching the pair of them. Instead, I went down to the locker room and with a black felt-tip pen wrote GET A LIFE! all across the front of Bonehead's locker. Big, so everyone could see it. That made me feel good, that did. That gave me a lot of satisfaction. It also made me late for maths, but like Noah I didn't give a damn.

When I got home I found that Noah had got there before me. He was talking to Mum in the front room and I didn't reckon he'd thank me for barging in, so I went round to talk to Rosa. I told her all that had happened, Fanny's bullshit speech and Noah's dramatic interruption, and she cried, 'That is just so cool!'

I told her that that was what Mark had said.

'Well, it is!' she insisted. 'To do a thing like that – in front of the whole school! Don't you think it's cool?'

I mumbled that I supposed it was. I guess in truth I was still trying to get my head round things.

'You only *suppose*?' said Rosa. 'I'm telling you, it was! It's just about the coolest thing I ever heard!'

'You don't sound very surprised,' I said.

She wrinkled her nose, as if considering the matter.

'I am sort of. It's just that it doesn't strike me as any big deal. You know?'

I grunted, in a Neanderthal way.

'It doesn't bother you, does it?' said Rosa. 'I mean…how do you feel?'

'I feel OK,' I said.

'You should! After all, what's changed? He's still Noah.'

'I told you,' I said, 'I feel OK!'

She looked at me, slyly.

'It doesn't make you want to throw up?'

I felt my cheeks go red. She didn't have to remind me of that! I told her, quite proudly, how I'd written GET A LIFE on Bonehead's locker.

'Did you sign it?' said Rosa.

'No,' I said, 'but he'll know it's me.'

And I still didn't give a damn!

Noah wasn't there when I arrived back home. Mum said he'd wanted to go and see Lars's parents. She asked me, just like Rosa had, how I was feeling, so I told her what I'd told Rosa, that I felt OK. I felt relaxed.

'It's cool,' I said.

'Are you sure?'

'See, what he did,' I said, 'it was like…well! Like sticking up for Lars. The only person who ever did so!'

'It troubles him,' said Mum, 'that he didn't do it sooner.'

I pointed out that the rest of us hadn't done it at all.

'Yes, and to that extent,' agreed Mum, 'we must all bear some share of the responsibility. We all failed him – we all let him down. But it's obviously a hundred times worse for Noah.'

I said that I could see that, and Mum said, 'Just as long as it's not going to make any difference between the two of you.'

That was the thing she was really anxious about. I assured her that it wouldn't.

'Noah's still Noah,' I said. 'It's no big deal.'

It is what I was truly trying to believe. So, OK! My big brother didn't go for girls. So what? So he fancied guys; it wasn't the end of the world. It was just going to take a bit of getting used to. That was all.

I said this to Mum. 'Not the end of the world,' I said.

'Exactly!' said Mum, sounding relieved. 'I'm so glad that's the way you see it!'

And then she told me that Noah wanted to talk to me, and I got a bit apprehensive about that. A bit hot and bothered. I went up to my room and messed about on the computer and wished the whole thing could be over with. I didn't want Noah talking to me! I'd heard what he'd got to say; what else was there? But Mum, however, seemed to think it was something he needed to do, and I felt she'd be upset if I said no.

'It's been really bad for him, Joel! If you feel

rough, just imagine how he must be feeling.'

I remembered again the day he'd told me about being in love.

'It's great, isn't it? Being in love!'

He'd been so happy! And then it had all gone sour, because Lars wanted to make a stand, while Noah just wanted to keep quiet. I couldn't help wondering how I would feel if I'd let Rosa down and simply stood by while everyone called her names and chalked obscenities about her in public places. I thought that I would feel like a traitor. So when Noah knocked on my door, a couple of hours later, I knew that I had to be brave and let him say whatever it was that he wanted to say.

All it was, was sorry.

'I'm sorry, kiddo! I'm really sorry! I've gone and dropped you in it, haven't I?'

'Me?' I said. 'I'm all right!'

'They're not giving you a rough time?'

'N-no,' I said. 'N-not really.'

'What does that mean?' said Noah.

'Well – you know!' I didn't want to go into details 'Just the usual idiots, but I can deal with them. No problem!'

'You sure?'

'Yeah,' I said. 'positive!'

'Mum's asked me if I'd like to transfer to sixth-form college for my last year.'

'Are you going to?'

'I don't know.'

I said, 'I would!'

'Why?' Noah perched himself on the edge of my desk. 'You think they'll give me the same treatment they gave Lars?'

'No. They reckon you deserve a medal for standing up to Fanny. But – well! I mean—'

'Anything's better than Hadley? You're probably right. You could go and join Rosa at Combe Cross, if you wanted.'

'Really?' I sat up at that. 'Did Mum say I could?'

'It's up to you. The choice is yours.'

'What are you going to do?'

'I haven't made up my mind. I think – probably—' Noah picked up a rubber band and began very slowly and carefully to wind it round a finger. 'Probably I'll…stay on.'

'Stay on at Hadley?'

He shrugged.

'After all that's happened?'

'I know; it sounds crazy. But I just feel—' he wound the rubber band more tightly. 'I just feel that – if I leave – it'll be like – letting them win.

Like...what Lars did – what he tried to do –
coming out – making a stand – like it was all for
nothing. No reason. You know what I mean?'

'Mm. I guess.'

'I'm not explaining it too well. It's just...he
wanted us both to come out. It was very important
to him. He didn't see why we should have to slink
around like criminals. Like it was something to be
ashamed of. He said sooner or later, you had to
make a stand. The two of us, together. Only I was
too much of a coward! I knew what it would be
like. I mean, I've been at Hadley since I was a kid.
Lars didn't realise. He thought I was
exaggerating.'

I nodded, man to man. I felt I had to be adult
about this. Noah was talking to me seriously, like
we were equals.

'I guess they're more relaxed about these things
in Sweden,' I said.

'It's possible. He just had no idea what this lot
could be like. I mean, Fanny...we've lived with
him! We know he's a redneck.'

'Bigoted old blimp.'

'And the rest. I tried to warn Lars, but...he was
set on it. He said if I wouldn't do it, he'd do it by
himself. I told him—' I saw the tip of Noah's

finger turning slowly purple as the rubber band bit into it. 'I told him, if he did, he'd…be on his own. I told him, I wasn't ready for this! I didn't know he'd come to see Mum. I thought I'd managed to talk him out of it. If he'd only waited!'

I watched in a kind of fascination as the tip of Noah's finger changed from deepest purple to fungus white.

'I might – maybe – have…come around to his way of thinking. I mean, I did agree with him! In principle. It was just – lack of balls is what it comes down to. I honestly never thought he'd go through with it! And then we had the talk, and—' Noah rolled the band back off his finger. His finger was all in ridges. 'And that was it. He just came out with it. In front of everyone. And I stood by and did nothing. Absolutely nothing! Worse than that. I turned my back on him. Just left him on his own to get on with it.'

Noah said I might not believe it, after all that stuff he'd given me about being in love – 'And I was!' he said. 'We were! It was the first time, for me. It hit me pretty hard. I guess up until that point, I'd thought I was immune. But, anyway—'

Here he stopped, like he was finding it really hard to go on. I thought back to Christmas Day. I remembered Lars calling round, and him and Noah going off together. I remembered things I hadn't even realised I'd noticed – looks that had passed between them, the way they had smiled at each other. And I think it was then, in that moment, that I finally accepted the truth: Lars and Noah had been in love, just the same as me and Rosa were. It was something I'd never quite been able to get my head round before. Or maybe I just hadn't wanted to. I don't know. But looking at Noah, as he was now, I could no longer doubt it.

Anyway, said Noah, after Lars had come out they'd had this big bust-up. Noah had been mad at him for going ahead when he thought they'd agreed not to. He'd got on his high horse.

'I gave him all this shit about...not wanting to be tarnished. Told him –' Noah's lip curled – 'told him I had my image to think of.'

I wasn't going to blame him; I could relate to that. I knew what it was like.

'Images are important,' I said.

'Images should reflect the truth,' said Noah. 'That was all Lars wanted...just to be true to himself. I realise—' he started with the band again, winding it back round his finger. 'I realise it's difficult for you to accept, but – the fact is, you don't – *choose* – to be gay. Or straight. It's just – what you are. And if you can't be – what you are – it means a whole part of your personality is being – suppressed. So my – *image* – that I was so concerned about, was just – a facade. I was so used to – living with it, I was…scared of coming out and just – being myself. If I'd just had the guts to stand by him—'

He twisted the band, looping it round and around. 'He might still be alive! We could have seen it through. The two of us. It was just – on his own, he – couldn't hack it. It was like I'd – betrayed him. You know?'

I tried to think of something to say, but nothing came.

'I wish you wouldn't keep doing that,' I said.

'Sorry!' Noah rolled the band off again and dropped it on the desk. 'I'm really sorry – for everything.' He gave me a wry sort of grin. 'You'll never be able to look at me the same way again, will you?'

'Doesn't make any difference to me,' I said. I really, really felt that. Like Rosa had said, Noah was still Noah. He was still my big brother who had stuck up for me and protected me when I was a kid.

'So how about Combe Cross? What do you reckon?'

'I dunno,' I said. It was a great temptation. 'What are you going to do?'

'I reckon I'll probably stay on. But that's no reason for you to do so! I'm the last person that should be influencing anyone.'

'I don't feel that way,' I said. 'I feel dead proud of you! Laying into Fanny like that...that'll go down in history, that will!'

It was the second time we'd been close. It hasn't happened again, but one day perhaps it might. I'd really like that.

Rosa has asked me how I'm going to end this book. She says the way a book ends is just as important as the way it begins.

'I suppose I ought to tie up any loose bits and pieces,' I said.

'Absolutely!' said Rosa. 'People will want to know what happens.'

But nothing really happened after my talk with Noah.

'You mean, that is THE END?' said Rosa.

I'd thought it was, but Rosa said, 'What about you?'

I said the story wasn't about me, but she said,

'Of course it is! You're the one that's telling it, aren't you?'

Only I've already told it – all the things that happened, and how Lars turned our lives upside down and made me re-think my prejudices.

But anyway. Noah stayed on at Hadley. Mum didn't want him to, she said he'd done his bit, he'd made his stand, but Noah insisted. He said it was something he had to do. I think he felt it was the only thing that made any sense of Lars's death. He felt that he owed it to him; and in the end Mum was forced to agree.

Fanny got the sack, just as Mark had predicted. He was removed by the Board of Governors and a new head took his place. Guess what? A woman! Oh, and next year there are going to be *girls* in the sixth form. Civilisation has arrived! And you could say that it was all due to Lars. Rosa says he left the world a better place – or at least, our small corner of it.

I have tried pointing this out to Noah, in the hope of solacing him, but he only mutters that if that is so then Lars paid a heavy price for it. I know he still feels terrible, and that it will be a long time, if ever, before he stops trying to shoulder all the blame. But I think that sooner or later he has to forgive himself. I'm sure Lars would forgive him! After all, he stood up before the whole school – and he stayed on, when he could have left. That has got to count for something.

I stayed on, too. I reckoned if Noah could do it, so could I. It was like Noah felt he owed it to Lars, and I felt I owed it to Noah. Lars had found the courage to make a stand, and so, in the end, had my brother. Now it was my turn.

Noah says I must be mad.

'You didn't have to do this,' he says.

But I wanted to. I keep thinking of Lars, standing up for Mr Ansari.

'Prejudice is everywhere – and it is always gross.'

When I think of that, staying on at Hadley seems like no big deal.

More Orchard Black Apples

☐ *Just Sixteen*	Jean Ure	1 84121453 1	£4.99
☐ *Love is for Ever*	Jean Ure	1 86039 770 0	£3.99
☐ *Wising Up*	E. A. Blare	1 84121 557 0	£4.99
☐ *If Only I'd Known*	Jenny Davis	1 84121 789 1	£4.99
☐ *Little Soldier*	Bernard Ashley	1 86039 879 0	£4.99
☐ *Wolf Summer*	Andrew Matthews	1 84121 758 1	£4.99
☐ *No Way Back*	Linda Newbery	1 84121 582 1	£4.99

Orchard Black Apples are available from all good bookshops, or can
be ordered direct from the publisher:
Orchard Books, PO BOX 29, Douglas IM99 1BQ
Credit card orders please telephone 01624 836000
or fax 01624 837033
or e-mail: bookshop@enterprise.net for details.

To order please quote title, author and ISBN
and your full name and address.
Cheques and postal orders should be made payable to
'Bookpost plc.'
Postage and packing is FREE within the UK
(overseas customers should add £1.00 per book).

Prices and availability are subject to change.